M000077194

The Feast

And other Horrifying Tales

By David Vorhees

Edited by Amy McCarthy

Cover art by Amuson Oluwaseyi

New Year's Day

A New Year, A New Day, A New Life

1.

Bzzzzz. Bzzzzz,

He stretches over to turn off his alarm. He can't believe he forgot to turn it off again. It was a holiday after all, and he didn't have to work even if it was a Monday. He has been off work for the holidays for almost two weeks, and every day his alarm goes off. Every day he swears he is going to turn it off, and every day he forgets. Today he has a good reason to forget.

His head is pounding. He must have drank way too much last night. He reaches to the far side of the bed to find his wife and feels nothing but air. Then he thinks to himself, "Oh that's right she isn't here." He had momentarily forgotten that he took an Uber home from the party. He hadn't been feeling well and it was after midnight, so he decided to leave. She had wanted to stay a little longer, she was having a good time and it was rare that she got to let her hair down, so he left her the car and called an Uber to take him home. It was only a few blocks away.

He swung his legs over the side of the bed and headed for the bathroom. Man did he have to piss. He realized it was more than his head that was pounding; his whole body was sore. He remembered everything that had happened last night before and after he got home. It was one of his many curses. He couldn't get blackout drunk if he tried. He always remembered everything: everything he said, and more importantly, everything he did when he drank. After he was done pissing, he took out the Advil and downed four of them. He then brushed his teeth and got dressed for the day; nothing fancy just some jeans and a t-shirt.

As he made his way downstairs to find something to eat, he heard someone knocking at the front door. At first, he thought it might be Carla and maybe she lost her key, but he realized the key was on the ring with the car key. There was no way it would be her anyway.

2.

Knock. Knock. Knock.

As he opens the door, the first thing he thinks of is "Man is it bright." he sees the lady first. Her dark brown hair is pulled back in a bun and she is wearing a dark pant suit with a thick pea coat overtop. Her skin is tan, which is odd for this time of year He thinks, "She would be really pretty if she put on some make-up and let her hair down." There is a man behind her wearing a similar dark suit with a tie and a tan winter overcoat.

"May I help you?" he asks.

"Police," the woman says "I'm Detective Alvarez, and this is my partner Detective Jones. Are you Mr. Grant Curtis?

"Yes" he replies.

"May we come in?" she asks.

"Ok" he says as he opens the door wider to allow them in "Can I ask what this is concerning?"

"Sir, a Carla Curtis, I'm assuming your wife, was found last night behind the wheel of a black 2018 Lincoln MKZ registered to you." Detective Alvarez stated.

"Ok, yes that is my car. Is my wife alright?" he asks, trying to sound worried.

"The vehicle was found off the road in a ditch about 2 miles from here. An ambulance was dispatched. I'm sorry, but they pronounced her dead at the scene." the detective said looking away.

"Dead? No, she couldn't be dead! She was just a few blocks away! We were at a friend's house, a New Year's Eve party. I left early; I wasn't feeling well." he said covering his mouth with his hand. "If I would have stayed, she would be here now, alive. Why did she try to drive home? Why didn't she call me or an Uber? Why didn't she just stay at Shirley's?" he asked. He asked because he knew they would want to hear him ask. He knew they would want to see if he was visibly upset. The police didn't send a uniformed officer, they sent two detectives, which means they think something other than an accident happened and they want to see if he had something to hide. Well he wasn't going to show them anything but what he wanted them to see.

"Shirley?" she asks.

"Yes, Shirley Kaufman over at 12834 West Hamilton." he said.

"That was where the party was?" she asked

"Yes" he replied.

"Why weren't you with her?" Detective Jones asked, speaking for the first time.

"I was there, I left early, shortly after midnight, I wasn't feeling well, and she wanted to stay so I called an Uber." he said

"Can anyone verify this?" the detective asked. Grant came to a sudden conclusion; he didn't like Detective Jones at all. He was more like Detective Busy Body.

"Yes, there were like 20 people at the party and then there's the Uber driver. Let me get my phone and I will give you the info for him." he said and then went to his bedroom to get his phone. He had left it on his nightstand after he got up. Normally he carried it with him, but he forgot to take it after he got dressed. He grabbed his phone and hurried back to the two detectives. On his way back he heard it for the first time:

3.

He could hear music play, but it was barely audible He thought "he knew the song", but more importantly he knew that sound. It was his wife's ringtone. He heard that song every time someone called her or sent her a text for the last 6 years. God how he hated that song. He had begged her to change it, but it was her favorite song by her favorite artist and sometimes she would just let it ring so she could listen to the song. As he pulled the Uber info up on his phone and handed it to the pretty detective, he tried but couldn't figure out for the life of him where the song was coming from. He was sure he could hear it. Maybe the detectives had it, "that makes sense, since they are investigating her death," he thought.

"This seems unimportant, but do you guys have her cell phone on you?" he asked tepidly.

"Her cell phone?" Detective Alvarez asked. Her curiosity suddenly stirred.

"Yes, like I said it seems unimportant, but her family's numbers are in there. I don't have them in my phone, and I need to get ahold of them and let them know." he came up with that lie on the spot and was quite proud of himself for a minute.

"No, we don't and why don't you have your in-laws numbers in your phone?" Detective Busy Body asked.

"We aren't very close. To be honest they never really liked me much. They preferred her ex over me, and they let me know it." he said, this time being honest for the most part. His in-laws did not like him, and they did prefer her ex, Scott, but he did have their numbers in his phone.

"Well I can understand that and to answer your question, no we don't have it and I'm not sure it was at the scene either." Detective Busy Body said.

"All them other boys wanna wind you up and take you downtown
But you look like the kind that likes to take it way out
Out where the corn rows grow, row, row my boat
Floatin' down the Flint River, catch us up a little catfish dinner
Gonna sound like a winner, when I lay you down and love you right
Yeah, that's my kind of night!"

He heard it again and he watched as the detectives didn't make a sound or move to hear it better. He started to believe that they knew he had killed her, and they were setting him up. He also couldn't shake the thought "but what if they were telling the truth and didn't have the phone? Where could it be? Did he pick it up last night after the accident? He didn't remember, but if he did, why couldn't they hear it? It is barely audible so maybe they can't hear it or maybe they can, and they just want to see his reaction."

"Sir are you okay?" the pretty detective asks.

"Yes, maybe, I don't know. Maybe I need to sit down." he says making his way to one of the chairs. He is glad to see the pretty detective take the chair next to him, but "Detective Busy Body" also sat down across from him on the couch. *"Why can't they just leave."* he thought. He has stuff to do and if he doesn't call Sheryl soon, she will begin to wonder.

"Do you need us to call someone for you? A friend? A family member?" Detective Alvarez asked.

"No, I will be fine, it's just all of this is a bit overwhelming." he said. Besides he didn't have any family and only a very few friends, most of them were Carla's. who would he have them call? Sheryl, his mistress? He could see concern in her face, and he liked that. She had a soft, kind face like Carla did. He didn't realize it until this moment, but he was going to miss her. He did miss her.

"All them other boys wanna wind you up and take you downtown
But you look like the kind that likes to take it way out
Out where the corn rows grow, row, row my boat
Floatin' down the Flint River, catch us up a little catfish dinner
Gonna sound like a winner, when I lay you down and love you right
Yeah, that's my kind of night!"

He heard it again but this time it was louder. Surely, they must have heard it this time. He looked at them, one then the other - nothing. They didn't hear it. He put his head between his knees and tried to remember last night, tried to remember what happened to that damn cell phone.

4.

He remembered getting out of the Uber, entering the house, turning off the security alarm and watching as the Uber drove away. He then changed into his dark sweats and tennis shoes. He exited through the back door, not bothering to set the alarm as he went the three plus miles journey through the woods to his wife's best friend Shirley's house. Their properties bordered the same woods, but it was a large forest area. He had mapped out his path back in October before it really got cold, marking trees with chalk and wiping them off as he walked by. It took him a little over an hour to make the trip. He had hoped that she would still be there, he was actually worried that she had already left. She seemed concerned about him and it wouldn't surprise him one bit if she left to check on him. She loved him and he knew that, but he didn't feel the same about her. He did once, but not in a very long time. Then he met Sheryl and he knew what he had to do.

He thought about just leaving Carla, but he would have to pay so much in alimony. Plus, he would lose the house and pretty much everything, possibly Sheryl, and he wasn't taking that chance. He told no one of his plan, not even Sheryl, and over the last year he had worked it all out. He would leave the New Year's party they attended every year at Shirley's house He would make sure to take an Uber home so he would have a record of him leaving the party in case the police became suspicious. He would make the hike through the woods, hide in the backseat of the car and wait for her to leave. Once she got into the car, he would use the Chloroform he procured to knock her out, then he would bash her head in and wreck the car to make it look like she died driving home drunk, something she had done on one or more occasions. Then he would walk the rest of the way home and burn all of his clothes, shower and wait for everything to go down.

He remembered doing all of that, but he also remembers that after the accident he was way more sore and stiff than what he thought he should be. As he got out of the driver's seat and moved her body into the place he had just occupied, her phone fell to the ground and that song had started to play. That goddamn song.

"All them other boys wanna wind you up and take you downtown
But you look like the kind that likes to take it way out
Out where the corn rows grow, row, row my boat
Floatin' down the Flint River, catch us up a little catfish dinner
Gonna sound like a winner, when I lay you down and love you right
Yeah, that's my kind of night!"

Someone was calling her. He picked up the phone and looked at the caller I.D. It was Shirley. Probably calling to make sure she got home all right. "No Shirl, she didn't make it home alright." he said to the cold night as he tossed her phone back into the car.

5.

He tossed the phone back into the car! He clearly remembers that, but does he? He was sure he had but now he just didn't know. Is his memory messing with him? He started to question everything, was he wearing Gloves? "Gloves," he thought, "he didn't need to wear gloves. It was their car. His fingerprints would already be all over it, as would his DNA. Then he had a thought about her blood splatter- did he get any of it on him? Sure, he burned his clothes and took a shower, but blood doesn't wash off easily with just soap and hot water; at least that's what they say on all those crime shows they watch. *You gotta use bleach.*

*"All them other boys wanna wind you up
and take you downtown
But you look like the kind that likes to
take it way out
Out where the corn rows grow, row, row
my boat
Floatin' down the Flint River, catch us up
a little catfish dinner
Gonna sound like a winner, when I lay
you down and love you right
Yeah, that's my kind of night!"*

It was getting much Louder now, he thought. *There is no way they can't hear it now.* He looked at them and he saw their faces; they were both smirking at him now. *They knew, they just wanted him to say it. Those motherfuckers have been playing him from the start!* He watched all those cop shows, and they were pulling the oldest scam on him yet - good cop, bad cop. *Those motherfuckers! But he knew, he knew that's what they were doing, and he knew if they were resorting to that, then they had nothing.*

*"All them other boys wanna wind you up and take you downtown
But you look like the kind that likes to take it way out
Out where the corn rows grow, row, row my boat
Floatin' down the Flint River, catch us up a little catfish dinner
Gonna sound like a winner, when I lay you down and love you right
Yeah, that's my kind of night!"*

"Sir, are you ok? You don't look so good" Detective Alvarez asked him, but he could barely hear her over that Goddamn song. *Why won't she just answer her fucking phone!*

"All them other boys wanna wind you up and take you downtown
But you look like the kind that likes to take it way out
Out where the corn rows grow, row, row my boat
Floatin' down the Flint River, catch us up a little catfish dinner
Gonna sound like a winner, when I lay you down and love you right
Yeah, that's my kind of night!"

"ANSWER THE FUCKING PHONE, ALREADY! I KNOW YOU GOT IT, YOU'VE BEEN FUCKING WITH ME ALL MORNING, JUST ANSWER IT. IF YOU'RE WAITING FOR HER TO ANSWER IT, SHE WON'T BECAUSE SHE'S DEAD! AND I KNOW BECAUSE I MADE SURE SHE WAS DEAD BEFORE I LEFT HER ASS IN THE DITCH!" he yelled at the detectives. As he yelled the song stopped, and the cell phone went quiet.

6.

"Mr. Curtis you are under arrest for the murder of your wife, one Carla Curtis." Detective Busy Body said as the pretty detective cuffed his hands behind his back." You have the right to remain silent - something you probably should have exercised a moment ago - anything you say can and will be used against you in a court of law. You have the right to an attorney. If you are unable to afford an attorney, and by the looks of this place that will not be a problem for you, the court will provide one for you. Do you understand these rights as I have read them to you?" he asked, but they did not wait for an answer as they started to direct him towards their car.

"Looks like you were right Jones, I owe ya lunch." the pretty detective told her partner.

"I just want to know, was there a cell phone?" Jones asked his partner.

"Yeah, but as far as I know it's still with the car." she said.

The End.

Valentine's Day

Necrophilia- A Love Story

Chapter 1.

1.

Jonah wasn't what he considered to be an average man. In fact, Jonah believed himself to be far below average. He was short, a little under 5' 6", frumpy, not fat but not lean either and he never considered himself to be an attractive man. Jonah, who had unremarkable brown hair with brown eyes and wore thick glasses, always believed he was destined to be alone forever. In his almost 30 years, Jonah never had a girlfriend, and had only ever asked one girl on a date when he was 17, and she laughed as she said no. Jonah never asked anyone out again until now. One night 4 years ago, Jonah got exceptionally lonely and hired a prostitute to spend the evening with him. He took her out to dinner and then to a fancy hotel. After they entered the room the young woman took off her clothes and kissed him. Jonah got so nervous and darted out of the room and ran back to his little one-bedroom house in embarrassment. That night he cried himself to sleep and vowed to change, swearing he would never be that cowardly again. Today Jonah wasn't feeling cowardly or embarrassed. Today, Jonah was on cloud 9. He had never been happier in his whole life. It was Valentine's Day and for the first time ever, he had a date. Not just any date, but a date with the girl of his dreams. He remembered the day he first saw her 5 years ago on his first day of work.

The building was 20 floors and every office shared a single mail room which was in the basement. On the morning of his first day he was given a tour of the building by the mail room manager, Greg Johnson. As the tour went, Mr. Johnson explained to him what his job would be. He was shown where the mail came into the building every morning and how it was sorted. He would be responsible for all the offices on floors 14-20. New guys got the tops floors. He was shown the supply elevator that he and all the other mail boys would be using. It was on the 17th floor of the building when he first heard her laugh, a laugh that sent a shockwave up his spine. Then he saw her, and time seemed to stop.

They entered an advertising office through a set of double glass doors with the name McVay & Mason Media written in white block lettering. They pushed the cart loaded with mail through the doors. That's when he heard that angelic laugh for the first time. He would hear her laugh countless times over the years and it always made him smile, but that first time was special. He turned and saw her; she was coming out of an office across from the double doors. He just stood there watching her, he couldn't move. She was tall, taller than him at least, and he thought she moved with the grace of an angel. She had wavy blonde hair that curved and hugged her slightly round face. Her green eyes popped out at him when she looked their way as she exited the office. Her name was Elizabeth Shearing, but everyone called her Liz. Liz was fit and lean, and on the day of their first meeting he could see the shape of her athletic body in the tight blue dress she was wearing. Her skin was smooth and tan. He had never seen anyone as beautiful off the silver screen. He was damn sure no one ever existed that was as beautiful as her.

Over the next 5 years he would deliver mail and watch her, admiring her from afar. They would have very limited interactions which were consistently made up of her smiling, saying hi and asking about his day. He would then smile a sheepish smile back, nod, say ok and hand her the mail and be on his way. Rarely was he able to muster more than a word or two towards her at a time. Every Valentine's Day he would deliver her flowers with a handwritten poem expressing how he felt, signed - your eternal love. This year would be different. This year he finally got up the nerve to sign his name to the card. This year he would deliver the flowers to her home in person and wait for her to read the card, then he would ask her out. He just knew she wouldn't say no, how could she? He knew she liked him. He figured she had to - why else would she always talk to him and smile at him?

2.

Jonah had spent all day preparing the perfect date. He bought her Roses, a nice bracelet, a box of chocolates, and was preparing her favorite meal - Chicken Parmesan and garlic bread. He spent over a $100 on a bottle of Chateau Pontet-Canet, a French red wine. He wanted everything to be perfect for Liz. He even rented a tux.

He arrived at her door at 6:45 p.m. He was so nervous his hands were sweating. He knocked and when she opened the door, he dropped the flowers because he was so struck by her beauty. When she opened the door, she looked confused and asked why he was there. He started to stumble over his words and fumbled the flowers and chocolates. They bent down to pick the items up together, and while looking at the concrete path he asked her to dinner. She smiled at this and giggled a little. At that he felt an anger rise in him but when he looked at her all he could say was, "Wow, you look gorgeous." she was wearing a red dress that stopped a little above mid-thigh, was low cut front and back, and hugged her fit frame in all the right places. She wore her hair down with curls that just reached her shoulders, and red lipstick to match her dress.

"Thank you." he heard her say. He was full of fear and excitement as he awaited her answer. He didn't hear what she said next and could only remember escorting her to his van; a 1994 Chevy Astro van. He opened the door and helped her inside. He looked at her and said thank you before closing the door.

Chapter 2.

1.

Jonah fumbled with the keys as he tried to unlock the door. His face was flushed with embarrassment as he finally unlocked the door after what felt like forever to him. The house was lit by candles spread throughout and smelled like a small, cozy Italian restaurant. He showed her to the table and pulled out her chair so she could sit. He then went to the kitchen and brought out their pre-prepared plates. There was a small vase with a single rose in the middle of the table and two long candles on each side. Next to the rose was a basket with garlic bread wrapped in a cloth napkin. Before he sat down, he turned on some music, a carefully prepared playlist he had made on his phone. He looked over the dining room; the music, the girl, and he had never felt such overwhelming happiness. He knew he may never be that happy again and he wanted it to last forever.

He made one last trip to the kitchen and grabbed a box of his special secret seasoning before he sat down. He asked her if she wanted some and when she shook her head, he proceeded to put some on his food.

They talked very little as they ate. He was still very nervous and every now and again would ask her if she liked her food. Then his favorite song began to play. It was a well-known band in the area but unknown virtually everywhere else. The song was Shattered by O.A.R. and when he heard those first chords play, he stood up and asked her to dance.

He pulled her close to him and as they danced, his arms were around her waist and hers over his shoulders. He could feel his hands sweating from nerves, but when he looked into her eyes he relaxed, and he kissed her for the first time.

It was euphoric! He had never felt such a rush as that first kiss, his real first kiss. They kissed again and although he was not a big man, he picked her up and carried her to bed.

2.

As they lay there in bed kissing, he slowly slides his hand up her thigh and he looks at her. "This is my first time." he confesses to her, she smiles, and they kiss again. He slowly undresses her and starts to undress himself, and suddenly feels that this may be wrong. But one look at her, amazed by her naked body, all those feelings went away. He then lays on top of her and they begin to make love.

Afterwards they are lying in bed, her lying on her side and him behind her, spooning her. His arms holding her tight, he thinks this is a love that songs and stories will be written about. This is one of the greatest love stories in history. Jonah and Liz together forever as written by the stars. He thinks about this and being together forever, even death won't keep them apart. He thinks of this and he falls asleep.

Chapter 3.

1.

As he pulls up to the small house, he feels an odd sense of foreboding. After 20 years as a cop, the last 10 as a detective, Sgt. Stephens knows that when he is called to a scene the day after a holiday, it is never a good thing. Since he became a homicide detective, any scene he gets called to is never a good thing.

He parks his unmarked, grey, police issued Ford POS along the curb directly across from the little house his GPS has led him to. As he exits the vehicle, he sees two uniformed officers roping the area off and the CSU van along with the Coroners van fighting for space in front of the house. He flashes a badge to a fresh-faced kid in a police uniform. "They keep getting younger looking or I'm just getting that much older," he thinks. As he enters the house, his partner of the last 2 years walks towards him. 'What we got Jones?" he asks.

"Well we got two bodies, naked, in the bedroom. Jones replies. Yesterday there was a report of an unknown man assaulting a woman, a Liz Shearing, and he was seen dragging her limp body from her house."

"The report actually says limp?" Sgt. Stephens asked.

"Yes, it does. Apparently, the witness, a Mrs. Abigail Wilson, Mrs. Shearing's neighbor from across the street, saw the unknown assailant that she described as a short roundish man putting her limp neighbor who looked asleep in a red and grey Chevy Astro van."

"Okay."

"This morning, while on patrol, a uniformed officer noticed a van fitting the description was parked in the driveway of this house. The officer parked, looked the vehicle over and proceeded to knock on the door. When he got no answer, the officer---

"Which officer?" Sgt. Stephens interrupts.

"Miller. The pup that checked your badge when you got here." Detective Jones said.

"Alright, continue." Sgt. Stephens added.

"Okay, after Miller got no answer, he decided to walk around the house and check things out. As he rounds the house into the back yard, he noticed two people laying in the bed naked. He knocked on the window and they did not stir. He knocked louder and yelled through the window. Nothing. He then proceeded to the back door, which he says was unlocked, entered and discovered the two were dead. He called it in and asked for a description of the abducted woman and realized she matched the description." Detective Jones said.

"So does CSU or the coroner have any idea what happened?" Sgt. Stephens asked.

"I'm so glad you asked. As you can see, there were lit candles that burned out during the night. A romantic dinner was set up but only one plate was eaten off of. CSU and the coroner, along with myself, have surmised that he attacked and possibly killed her when he abducted her, and he brought her back here for what looks like a romantic dinner for two. His food was covered in rat poison, which it seems he put on there. He then carried her dead body from the dinner table to the bedroom where he then sexually assaulted her post-mortem." Detective Jones said.

"Wait, he had sex with her corpse?" Sgt. Stephens asked.

"Looks like it. According to the coroners initial examination of her body, yes. He said there is significant damage to her genital area that definitely occurred after her death." Detective Jones said.

"Jesus, what a sick bastard. Who was this guy?" Sgt. Stephens asked.

"Jonah Richardson. He was 29 years old and lived at this address for the last 7 years. He worked in the mailroom of the same office building that our victim worked at." Detective Jones said.

"At least we know how he knew her." Sgt. Stephens said.

"I think it was more than that." Detective Jones said.

"How so?" Sgt. Stephens asked.

"We found a bunch of pictures of her at the park, her gym, in front of her house, and after doing a bank check we found that every year for the last five years he has been sending her flowers on Valentine's Day and her Birthday." Detective Jones said.

"So, this is a case of unrequited love, gone bad?" Sgt. Stephens asked

"Something like that. It is my belief he killed her at her house. The coroner believes she died by strangulation, and he then brought her corpse back here for a romantic, Valentine's Day dinner. Where he ate poison, he carried her to the bedroom to have sex with her corpse, and then died holding her." Detective Jones said.

"Sounds romantic in a sick kind of way. What is this world coming to when even love starts killing?" Sgt. Stephens pondered.

The End.

Easter

The Resurrection

Chapter 1

1.

He looked out over his congregation as he crossed the pulpit towards the altar. He loved to make an entrance and he loved the holidays. Easter and Christmas, he never worried about attendance. It was always standing room only. All eyes were on him and how he loved the attention, the rush of importance and power he felt as he stood before them and preached God's word. It was as if the Almighty was pouring through him and out towards the people. After all, this was a show and he was a showman at heart.

"Good Morning and Happy Easter to you all." he said. The whole of the church responded with Happy Easter in one glorious unified voice. As he reached the altar, he noticed three empty seats in the front row. The three seats were reserved for the Williams family and they never missed a service, especially a holiday service. He briefly contemplated what was wrong, maybe the young girl was sick or there was a family emergency. He made a point to write down on a piece of paper:

Check on Williams family after service concludes.

"God be with you", he said to the congregation as he looked up from the altar, not noticing the small plastic Easter egg sitting on the altar near his bible. *Let the show begin*, he thought. It wasn't that he was a non-believer or a charlatan. He believed whole heartedly in God and his good works. But he also knew that people didn't come to just hear him talk about God. They came for a show, to be entertained, and if he could spread God's word more effectively by being entertaining, then why the hell not. Better than the alternative - a boring preacher and an empty church. He put butts in seats and that mattered when spreading the good word.

"Today we come together not to remember the resurrection of Jesus Christ, our Lord and Savior, but to Celebrate and acknowledge his power over death itself. To worship him and God, and them showing us the undeniable proof of life after death. Easter is not about cute little bunnies that leave baskets full of candy and prizes, or about hidden plastic eggs from Walmart full of some unknown treasures." he says picking up the plastic egg on the altar and showing it to his audience. This is his audience, and this is his show. He briefly marvels at the weight of the egg and wonders what Stephanie put in it. "It's about faith and our faith in God's dominion over everything in this world, including death. It's about how he gave up his son for our sins and then brought him back to prove to us his true power. 1st Corinthians chapter 15 verse 3 through 8; For what I received, I passed on to you as of first importance: that Christ died for our sins according to the Scriptures, that he was buried, that he was raised on the third day according to the Scriptures, and that he appeared to Cephas, and then to the Twelve. After that, he appeared to more than five hundred of the brothers and sisters at the same time, most of whom are still living, though some have fallen asleep. Then he appeared to James, then to all the apostles, and last of all he appeared to me also...I ask you, why is the resurrection so important? And I tell you; because it establishes Jesus as a Lord, our Lord in Heaven. I have people ask me all the time if I ever wondered if the resurrection was a hoax, if his disciples found his tomb and removed his body. And I in turn ask them why they would do this. And they answer to perpetuate this grand hoax of resurrection and prove the prophecy that the man they follow is the one true Messiah. I ask them what prophecy? Then I inform them that there was no prophecy to the resurrection, they knew nothing of it and therefore would have no reason for perpetuating this grand hoax. They are left mouth open and dumbfounded with no argument left." he pauses briefly. "Acts chapter 2 verse 22 through 32 on the day of Pentecost ... Peter said: Fellow Israelites, listen to this: Jesus of Nazareth was a man accredited by God to you by miracles, wonders and signs, which God did among you through Him, as you yourselves know. This man was handed over to you by God's deliberate plan and foreknowledge; and you, with the help of wicked men, put Him to death by nailing Him to the cross. But God raised Him from the dead, freeing Him from the agony of death, because it was impossible for death to keep its hold on Him." he continued to preach as he opened the little, generic plastic egg and what he saw inside left him speechless.

2.

He noticed a tiny piece of paper wrapped around one end of the long round object in the plastic egg. The item was completely wrapped in a paper towel and was wet with a red pasty substance on one end that reminded him of ketchup. As he unwound the paper towel, he stopped talking. All breath had left him. He couldn't make a sound if he could think of something to say. He felt as if his body and brain were shutting down as he looked down at the amputated finger that was housed in the tiny plastic egg.

After a brief moment of staring silently at the finger, he began to recognize to whom it belonged. He saw the pastel blue polish on the nail and the large diamond carat engagement ring that was entwined with a white gold wedding band. He remembered the day it was put on the woman's finger, because he served as the officiant of her wedding. He also saw this ring every day, seeing as she worked for the church as its secretary. His secretary - Stephanie Williams. This finger belonged to her, and he then remembered that she and her family were not at service today.

Dear God, he thought. What is going on? He unfurled the piece of paper and read the note inscribed on it:

I'm sure you saw the finger and deduced who it belonged to. Tell no one, no cops, or I will kill the whole family. But it is Easter and Easter egg hunts were my favorite when I was young, so let's have a hunt shall we? I have placed 6 eggs all over the town, each with a clue and a surprise inside. Find the eggs, decipher the clues and find me by 5 p.m. tonight if you want the family to live. I believe that should give you about 8 hours. Good Luck.

Clue: Matthew chapter 27 verse 42 – He saved others, they said, but he can't save himself! He's the king of Israel! Let him come down now from the (Blank), and we will believe in him.

"Pastor Brian, is everything OK?" he heard Ryan ask as he hurriedly hid the contents of the egg.

"No, No I am... I am not feeling very well all of a sudden. Please take over, Ryan." he said.

"Yes of course, you look very pale, maybe you should go lie down." Ryan said.

"Yes, maybe I should." he lied, knowing full well where he was to go next. "My sermon is written on the paper under my bible, the scriptures are marked." He said.

"We will make do, just go lie down and feel better." Ryan said.

Ryan was fresh from seminary and was learning the ins and outs of running a church. He was a good young man and he knew that he would be fine. Ryan had led a few Sunday sermons since his arrival just before Halloween. He could hear Ryan explaining to the congregation why he was leaving and asked them to pray for him. He wanted them to pray for the Williams family, because he felt they needed it more than he did.

He walked to get his coat and keys, and then headed out the door of his office that lead to the staff parking lot where his car was located. He also grabbed a grey plastic bag that had 'Walmart' written on the front of it in blue lettering and placed the egg and its contents in the bag. He thought it fitting since that was most likely where the egg originated from. As he pulled out of the parking lot and headed towards the center of town, he was trying to figure out why this was happening. What could the Williams have done to deserve this? Why him and not a member of the police? He had heard of things like this happening in the movies and on TV, but he never thought they would happen to him. He remembered seeing a documentary on the History Channel once about the Zodiac killer in San Francisco that liked to tease the police with cryptic clues. He also knew the Zodiac Killer was never caught, but he is not a policeman and he tried to think of any cause as to why this was happening and why now.

As he parked along the side of the road next to the town park and got out of the car, he recalled an incident that happened nearly 10 years ago but thought it couldn't be related. Everyone involved in that was dead except himself.

As he passed the large gazebo, he saw what had brought him to the park. In the center of it all stood a 20-foot cross. He remembered when the town put that cross up 20 years ago. Nowadays that wouldn't happen even in a small town like Maple Grove, but then not only did it happen, but the whole town attended the event and watched with joy at the unveiling of the monument. He walked towards it and saw immediately what he was looking for: a light pastel pink plastic egg sitting on the base of the cross.

He opened the egg hesitantly and saw it was similar to the one from the church. It had a small piece of paper wrapped around an object in a blood-soaked paper towel. He unwrapped the object and saw it was an ear. It was Steph's ear. He recognized the gold cross earring she wore every Sunday. He sat down and tears flowed from his eyes. He could feel the guilt and knew he was responsible for all of this. He had hoped he was mistaken about the finger, but this was her ear. He knew because of how many times he had kissed this very ear in his office, his home, and even a few motel rooms they snuck off to once in a while.

Chapter 2.

1.

He wiped his eyes and put the contents of the egg and the egg itself into the plastic bag, except the little piece of paper with the clue written on it that he unraveled and read.

Clue 2: James Chapter 3 Verse 1-2: Not many of you should become teachers, my brothers, for you know that we who teach will be judged with greater strictness. For we all stumble in many ways. And if anyone does not stumble in what he says, he is a perfect man, able also to bridle his whole body.

He wondered what this clue meant. He wondered if this was a comment on his behavior with the married Stephanie Williams. He decided to go to the Williams' house and see what was going on there. He figured the person behind this sick Easter egg hunt must be Greg her husband. He must have found out about them. He wondered if he knew about the girl, the girl he called daughter, the girl who is supposed to celebrate her 11th birthday in a few months' time.

2.

As he was driving down the side streets towards the Williams' home, he recalled the first time he and Stephanie kissed and how the whole sordid affair began.

It was a Wednesday night and they were cleaning up after an AA meeting. He looked over at her as she was cleaning up the coffee machine. He watched her as she moved gracefully from one task to another. He could see the shape of her well-toned thighs through her skirt, and saw how small her waist was where the skirt belt tightened with half her blouse tucked in. She was 5'9", tall for a woman, and completely beautiful with her curly golden locks that came down and hugged her round face. She took very good care of herself, but he noticed this evening she had not bothered with any make-up, which he thought made her even more beautiful. He could also see that her eyes were puffy and figured she had been crying earlier. He had also noticed that she was quiet and had not been her usually smiling and jovial person today.

"You gonna tell me what's wrong, or do I have to guess?" he asked her.

"Nothing, nothing is wrong." she lied without looking up at him.

"I know you have been crying, I am your friend and your pastor, its ok to talk to me. I just wanna help." he assured her.

She stopped cleaning and looked up at him. He saw the tears streaking down her face as she walked towards him and hugged him. "It's Greg. We got into this huge fight and now I don't know what do." she said.

"It's just one fight. I don't know what it was about, but it's not the end of the world." he told her. "You guys will get through this."

"It's not just one fight. We have been at each other's throats for months now. Last night was just... it was the worst one yet." she said lowering her head and looking away so he couldn't see her tears. "Last night he left, and he hasn't been back since. He hasn't even called."

"Have you tried to call or text him?" he asked.

"I did. It went to voicemail and he hasn't texted back." she replied.

Over the next few hours she would talk, and he would listen. She would tell him about the fights, how they started, and what they were about. She would confide in him her fears of her husband having an affair. They were sitting in his office on the couch he kept in there and at one point they were holding each other as she cried. When she looked up, they stared into each other's eyes. He used his thumb to gently wipe away the tears from her face and they kissed.

The kiss seemed to last forever before they started to undress each other. That night they made love for the first time. The next day Greg came home and apologized. She told him about their talk and how he wants to work it out. She told him and then told him she wanted to feel the way he made her feel the night before and they made love for the second time on his couch. Over the next few months they would touch and steal away moments with each other. They would catch themselves staring at each other for long periods of time before forcing themselves to look away. Each night she would go home wanting to be in his arms again and he would watch her leave, wishing she could stay a little longer.

One evening he admitted to her that he had fallen in love with her and she had said she felt the same way. He told her he hadn't felt that way about anyone in a very long time, around 11-12 years to be exact. That was 2 days ago on Good Friday. She told him she would talk to Greg and leave him after the holiday, but maybe she couldn't wait any longer. Maybe she told him, and he went nuts and started to cut her up and leave pieces of her in plastic eggs to punish them.

3.

When he pulled into her driveway, he saw her Kia Sorento parked just outside of the closed garage door. He got out and walked to the door wondering where Greg's Black Chevy Silverado was. As he approached the door, he saw that the house looked quiet and dark as if no one was home. He figured that it would be too easy to find them there, Greg had to have taken them somewhere else. But why the girl? Why would he want to hurt the kid? Did she see him hurt her mom and figured he couldn't leave any witnesses? Maybe, but something was wrong, and he knew it.

He rang the bell, but no one answered. Then he knocked, shouted and knocked and still nothing. He tried the door and it was locked, so he peered into the windows and he could see the back-sliding door looked to be broken. He walked around the house and entered through the broken glass door. As he stepped through the door he could feel and hear the glass crunch under his shoes. He looked around and saw signs of a struggle, and then he saw another sign written in what looked like blood on the wall.

GET BACK TO THE HUNT

YOURE WASTING TIME

I HAVE ALL 3 OF THEM

THEY WILL DIE AT MIDNIGHT

IF YOU DON'T FIND US FIRST.

He has all three of them. He wonders what that means. It means Greg is a victim and not the one behind this maniacal Easter egg hunt. He wonders who is then? He wonders who else did they - he - offend this much? His mind again wonders back in time to a memory, but he pushes it aside once more with the thought of all of them being dead and no one else knowing. But somebody must, he thinks. Somebody must know, but who? And if they did, why wait so long? Did they wait because they couldn't find him, or have they been watching him and waiting for him to repeat his sins?

He pushes the thoughts out of his mind again and pulled the little note with the clue back out and read it again. He recognized this scripture from a sermon he gave before Christmas; it was a message to students and teachers. With all the teachers who have been on the news lately for having sex with students, he wanted to put out a message to those who were thinking about crossing the line and to keep them on the straight and narrow, a path he himself had trouble walking at times. He then remembered that Stephanie was also a substitute teacher for the local high school and was working there because Mrs. Miller, the English teacher, was on maternity leave. He rushed back out to his car and headed for the school.

4.

The school was unlocked as there were some people getting the gym ready for the Easter egg hunt and play they put on every year. They held it at the school because the church was way too small to accommodate everyone that would show up. People from all over town showed up for this, even the ones who weren't holy or who just didn't go to church.

Her room was right around the corner from the office and it was also unlocked. As he opened the door, he noticed that there was tape covering the lock which was preventing it from latching. The door usually locked every time they left the room and could only be opened from inside or with a key. A safety measure the school board had implemented because of the rash of school shootings throughout the country.

He didn't focus too long on the tape but instead walked into the room and quietly closed the door. He turned around and saw it immediately; an orange plastic egg sitting right in the center of her desk. He stood there, fear overcoming him. He feared what he would find in the egg this time, another finger, the other ear, maybe a nose - her nose. He didn't like thinking about it like that. Her finger, her ear, always her. What they did was wrong, but she didn't deserve this. No one did.

He steeled himself and started to walk slowly towards the desk. Towards the egg. Towards what new hell awaited him in that seemingly innocent plastic oval. He picked up the egg and cracked it open and saw a familiar sight. He pulled off the paper towel and uncovered the secret it was hiding. A toe. A little toe, most likely the pinky toe. He could tell it was a woman's toe, but not if it was Steph's or the kid's. He sat it down and opened the note.

Clue 3: Jeremiah chapter 33 verse 6: Behold, I will bring to it health and healing, and I will heal them and reveal to them abundance of prosperity and security.

He read the note and read it again. He sat down in her chair. He sat there trying to find meaning in this scripture. He was trying to find his meaning in this scripture. He sat there for what seemed like forever but to no avail. He sat there and worried about the woman he loved, her husband and their child. He sat there and worried he was not capable of solving this clue. He sat there and read and reread the scripture over and over again. He couldn't make heads or tails of it. He knew the scripture but not well.

He pulled out his phone and typed the scripture into the search engine on google.

As he scrolled through the plethora of websites that Google had found, he saw no real continuity except that all started with health and cure. He thought about those words until his head hurt, "I need some Advil" he thought. A drug that would stop the headache he was getting. A drug from a drugstore. A drugstore - no, that wasn't right. He wrote the words down on the dry erase board behind him and tried to work it out. He thought about drugstores again but thought people don't go to drugstores to get cured, they go to hospitals. Maple Grove doesn't have a hospital, but it does have an ambulatory care center, a satellite of the big catholic hospital in Lima. He also knew there was a chapel in the ambulatory center for he had a key. He and Stephanie had met there a few times. He hurried to the door but opened it slowly and cautiously as he peered his head out to see if anyone was around. He didn't see anybody and wasn't sure what he would say if he did, especially since he was supposed to be giving a sermon right now or at the very least laying down on the couch in his office.

On his way to the hospital he was trying to think of a good excuse as to why he wasn't at the church. He parked his car and sat there thinking of what to say to avoid arousing suspicion when his phone rang, and he nearly jumped out of his skin. He picked up his phone and read the caller ID. It was Ryan. Was service over already? He checked the time and it was a little past one. Not only had service been over for more than an hour, but he also had 5 missed calls from Ryan. He answered it, "Hello".

"Hello, Minister. After service ended, I went to check on you in your office and you weren't there. I have called repeatedly. We are all very worried about you, are you ok?" His voice was full of concern and he knew it was genuine. Ryan was one of the truly unselfish men in the world.

"Yes, I'm fine. I couldn't get comfortable, so I went home." he lied.

"I checked your house and you weren't there." Ryan inquired worriedly.

He couldn't see any reason to lie to Ryan again, so he said, "No, I was there but I started to feel worse, so I am now at the hospital." he said honestly.

"Oh, well is everything alright?" Ryan asked.

"I haven't seen the doctor yet but I'm sure it's nothing major, when I know I will call and let you know, ok?" he said.

"Yes, ok. Thank you and feel better soon alright." Ryan said.

"Alright I'm sure I will. Bye." and with that he hung up the phone, without waiting to hear Ryan repeat the word bye back to him as is customary.

With the service over all he has to do is walk in and head straight to the chapel. If anyone does question him, all he has to say is he is picking something up and that would be the truth. On his way to the chapel he said hi to three people; 1 doctor and 2 nurses, and not one of them looked at him curiously as to try and figure out why he was there on Easter Sunday.

Even though he was in the clear, he opened the door to the chapel slowly as if it was booby-trapped and looked around for witnesses to his strange behavior before entering the room. The room was small even as far as hospital chapels go. It had a red wall to wall carpeting and three rows of padded, foldable chairs with 3 of them on each side of a center aisle. At the back of the room was a small statue of Jesus and a small podium that acted as the altar. The wall was painted white with maroon curtains hanging behind the podium, and right in the center of the aisle was a blue plastic egg.

6.

As he bent down and picked up the egg, he heard the door to the chapel open behind him. He quickly stood and turned to see an older woman standing before him.

"Oh, excuse me, I thought I could be alone here." she stated.

"No, please." he said, gesturing towards a chair. "Please, have a seat. I was just leaving." he said pocketing the egg and feeling the weight of it as it hit the bottom of his pocket.

"Oh, its fine, I was just looking for a place to gather myself."

"Ma'am is everything alright? My name is Pastor Brian White, and if you need help by all means I am here for you." he said and this he said with all of his heart. One of the true joys he ever felt as a pastor, besides spreading God's word, was helping people through difficult situations. It was a similar situation that made him decide he wanted to be a pastor in the first place.

"My husband is going in for surgery and I..." She stumbles over her tears to get the words out, "I am very scared."

"Would you like me to pray with you?" he asks, and she agrees wordlessly. "Can you tell me a bit about him?"

"Well his name is James and he is 66 years old. This is his first surgery ever, crazy as that sounds." she laughs a little.

"What is he having surgery for, if you don't mind me asking?" he said

"No, I don't mind. He is having an emergency bypass; open heart surgery." she says trying not to break down and cry. "They had to call in a special heart doctor from Lima to perform the surgery. They said he was too weak to transport him. We were getting dressed for service this morning when I found him lying on the bathroom floor barely breathing. The ambulance driver said he looked like he had a major heart attack and was lucky to still be alive."

"How long have you been married?" he asks.

"Going on 43 years next month." she says.

"That's amazing." he replies with admiration.

"It wasn't always easy. We started dating in high school. I was a doe-eyed freshman and he was a sophomore and a star football player already. All the girls had a big crush on him. I remember the first time I saw him, standing in the hallway next to his locker with his football buddies all around him. He was so handsome standing there. I remember he looked at me and smiled, and I got so nervous I just looked down at the floor and kept walking." she continued. "He thought I didn't like him, and he told me later that it made him notice me even more. For the next two weeks he kept trying to talk to me and I wouldn't say a word to him. I was too nervous you see; big, handsome, popular football star and little ol me. When he asked me out for the first time I almost died." she continued, and he just watched her with awe and admiration, her eyes lighting up as she remembered and talked about the past. "When he did ask me out finally, I couldn't say a thing. Thankfully my best friend Sondra was there and said yes for me. He once told me he thought I was mute and couldn't talk, but on that first date we talked for hours as if we had known each other our whole lives. I still think that was the moment we fell in love. Over the next three years we were mostly inseparable, except for when we fought and boy, we had some doozies back then. Then he graduated and joined the Navy. Four years later, he came home and got a job at the little factory here in town. I guess it's not so little anymore, and we were married not long after." she concluded.

"Wow, that is an amazing story." he said. Listening to her brought up a flurry of his own emotions about Steph, even though it was wrong that he did love her. Maybe even as much as this little old woman loved her James. He also thought of Melissa and his heart began to ache. He still mourned her and as his first true love he figured he always would. "Let us Pray." he said as he took her hand and they bowed their heads." Dear heavenly Father, I am here today on this holy day with." he stops and realizes he never asked her name.

"Evelyn." she said.

"With Evelyn, and we are praying for the safety of her beloved James. As you know Father, James is having a heart surgery as we speak, and we pray in Your name and the name of Your one and only Son Jesus Christ who was risen today. Please give James the strength to survive this and give the doctor a steady hand coupled with your guidance to see him through. We pray in your name, Amen."

"Thank you." she cried.

"Would you like me to stay a little while longer with you?" he asked.

"No, please go on and thank you. It may sound silly but that really helped. I needed that; I just didn't know how much." she said.

"It's not silly at all and you're welcome. God knew what you needed, and he has a way of bringing folks together when they need it the most." he said as he was getting up to leave. "Take care and God bless you. I hope all goes well. I will continue to pray for you and your husband."

"Thank you and I will pray for you as well. You seem like you need it too." she replied in kind and he said to himself - *you don't know how much I do.*

7.

He thought about Evelyn and James all the way back to his car. He thought about their story and how he would tell the story of the two women he loved in his life. Would he tell people that he met them at church? Yes. Would he tell them he fell in love with them almost instantly? Yes. Would he tell them that both were happily married when he met them and that one had died because of him? On that he felt he would say no.

Sitting in his car he dug the plastic egg out of his pocket and opened it. he was starting to get used to finding gruesome objects in the eggs and he figured he would find another finger, the other ear, maybe even a toe, but he was not prepared for what he saw when he unwrapped the paper towel.

At first, he was unsure of what he was staring at when he finished unwrapping his prize. He looked at the fleshy discolored objects and realized they were barely connected by a small piece of flesh at each end. He picked it up and when he pinched the object closed, he knew immediately what he was holding.

He sat there holding it between his forefinger and thumb. He sat there looking at it in shock and horror, he sat there for a long while after he realized he was holding her lips. For a moment he couldn't think and when he finally had a thought, all he could think about was the bastard that cut off her lips. He wondered how many times he kissed those lips, how many times he had rubbed his thumb and finger along them, how many times she had smiled at him and kissed him with them as he sat there holding her lips in his hand, between his fingers. He began to cry.

8.

After what seemed like an eternity, he wrapped the pair of lips, "her lips" he thought, back up in the paper towel, enclosing them back in the egg and putting them with the finger and ear in the plastic bag. He then opened the little piece of paper and read the next clue:

Clue 4: Peter chapter 2 verse 13-14: Submit yourselves for the LORD's sake to every human authority: whether to the emperor, as the supreme authority, or to governors, who are sent by him to punish those who do wrong and to commend those who do right.

He figured this one out relatively quickly. The next egg was at city hall, but where in the 3-story building was the small plastic egg and what would be inside it when he found it? He thought about the building and realized there was nothing there that was connected to the church. The town abided by the constitution and kept the state separate from the church. He thought of the court rooms, the title office and all that was inside, and then realized today was Sunday and city hall would be closed and locked up tight. He thought he wouldn't be able to put a little tape over a latch this time because the county Sheriff's Department was posted at the building during working hours. They also did an inspection checking all the doors and locks before leaving each night. The building was also located next door to the police station and would be very difficult to break into without being noticed. Then he remembered the church had donated a bench last Memorial Day in honor of town members who lost their lives serving in the military. He started the car and headed downtown.

When he got to the bench in front of city hall, he saw no egg and instantly panicked. What if a cop had found the egg with a bloody, separated body part contained inside? What if a child found it? He dropped to his knees and began to search frantically, and then he saw it. Taped to the bottom of the bench like in a spy movie was the bright pastel green egg. He quickly ripped the egg from under the bench and pocketed it, hoping no one was watching from the building next door.

After getting back into his car he removed the tape carefully from the egg and held it closed in his hand. He thought if he didn't open it then maybe this wasn't really happening and that the only way this continued was if he kept playing along. He knew that thinking was folly and whatever this egg contains was in there whether he opens it or not. She is suffering whether he plays or stops, but if he stops, she dies for sure along with her family. If she is not already dead. He doesn't want to be held responsible for the death of three women he loves.

9.

He opened the egg hurriedly. He wanted this over and over now. It was closing in on 3 o'clock and he still had one more egg to find, one more clue to decipher and a maniac to stop. He pulled out the paper and two small, rubbery round objects fell out of the egg. At first, he thought they were pieces of pepperoni. It wasn't until he looked to where they landed on his lap that he realized they were nipples. Her nipples. He wasn't sure they were hers, but all the other parts were, so why should this be any different? This maniac was punishing them for their affair. For both his affairs. He picked the nipples up horrified and placed them back in the egg with the others and read the clue.

Clue 5: Psalm chapter 82 verse 3-4: Defend the weak and the fatherless; uphold the cause of the poor and the oppressed. Rescue the weak and the needy; deliver them from the hand of the wicked.

He knew this verse very well; he had done many sermons speaking for the orphanage in town and trying to get people to give money to support it, but he knew this was not the orphanage he was supposed to go to. He knew it was the orphanage in Toledo where his first church was located that he was supposed to go to. The orphanage where Melissa's daughter ended up after her mother's death because of him.

Chapter 3.

1.

As he turned north onto the interstate and began the hour or so drive to the orphanage in Toledo, he began to remember that fateful day when he lost his church, his love and his daughter.

It was 10 years ago on Easter Sunday and he had just walked into his office after Easter services ended and found Melissa and Celeste, their 8-month-old daughter, waiting for him.

"I told him last night." she started

"How much?" he asked.

"Everything. When the affair started, how it started, with whom." she looked at him sorrowfully. "And I told him about Celeste, that she wasn't his." she started to tear up at this.

"How did he take it?" he asked. His heart was breaking. He liked Kyle and never meant for any of this to happen, but it did, and they were in love and now they had a child together as well. He also knew that she loved Kyle and never wanted to hurt him, but she loved him more and they wanted – needed - to be together, to be a family.

"Not well. He screamed and yelled, he threw things and broke things. I was truly scared of him. He never made me feel that way before and I am afraid of what he would have done if not for her." she said.

"What do you mean?" he asked.

"I thought he was going to hurt me; I truly believed he was, but she started crying and that seemed to snap him out of his rage. He left and I haven't heard anything from him. I called his parents, the bar he likes to go to and some of his friends and no one has heard from him." she said standing up and nearing him so he could wrap his arms around her and make her feel safe. "I'm still scared of what he might do, I've never seen him like this before."

"I'm sure he just needs some time to process this. He is probably somewhere crying and trying to come to terms with it. He will be fine, I'm sure of it." But he wasn't sure of it or anything. He knew a man that loses everything he holds dear can cause him to do drastic things. He wouldn't be surprised if he committed suicide and the police find his body in the next few days. He hoped it wouldn't come to that because he knew she would blame herself, hell she might even blame him and that could end their life together before it truly even begins.

2.

They spent the rest of the afternoon doing the egg hunt with the children, serving lunch, taking pictures of kids with the Easter bunny and of the whole congregation enjoying themselves, never once letting on what was going on behind the scenes.

Only after the last table was wiped down and put away, after the garbage was taken out and thrown in the dumpster, and after the last volunteer left for the night and they were finally alone did they allow themselves to show affection towards each other. It had been almost two years of sneaking around, stealing moments and finding ways to be with each other. It wasn't always difficult as his schedule was easily manipulated, and she had been active in the church for years prior to his arrival so seeing her there a lot was not unusual. The husband's work life kept him busy and out of town more often than not. He had come to realize that that work schedule caused her loneliness and had made room in her heart for them to get together. It wasn't easy at first, but the more they tried to deny their feelings for one another the stronger they got, until they couldn't hold back any longer. One night after an evening service they exploded into each other's arms and never looked back.

On this night, they had put Celeste down in her port-a-crib in his office and they were in the sanctuary wiping it down, when a man walked in and they knew right away who it was. Kyle was standing there in the doorway and he was obviously drunk with a bottle in one hand and a gun in the other.

"Well don't you two look happy, cleaning the Lord's house together. So Preacher, how many times did you fuck my wife on the altar right there?" he said drunkenly. "How many times did you two defile God's house with your sinful lust?"

"Kyle?" she questioned, "Kyle, I was so worried, I was..."

"SHUT YOUR WHORE MOUTH!" Kyle yelled.

"Kyle, calm down. We didn't mean to hurt you." he said.

"Hurt me? Hurt me preacher? Naw, you didn't hurt me, you just opened my eyes to the truth." Kyle said.

"The truth?" he asked.

"The truth about that slut bitch next to you and the truth that God doesn't exist because if he did, he would have struck you the moment you defiled this so-called house of worship." Kyle said.

He raised his hands and started to move towards him. "Now, that's close enough preacher." he said raising the gun. Kyle then took a long drink of the brown liquid with most of it going down his face and neck. He walked towards them, gun raised, liquid splashing out of the bottle. He pointed the gun right at his wife's pretty face. "I should just do the world a favor and end you right now. If we were in another country I would be within my legal rights as husband." Kyle stammered. "But I got other plans. Preacher, now I know you got some duct tape in that altar drawer right there."

"Yes, I do." he admitted.

"Good, glad you didn't lie to me. Now grab that chair right there and tape her up nice and good, and if you don't, I will kill her right now." He didn't even hesitate; he didn't want to give Kyle any inclination to shoot her before he can calm him down and figure a way out of this for everyone. Kyle was watching as he pulled the tape out of the drawer and grabbed the chair. He moved the chair behind Melissa and helped her sit down. He then began to tie her up. She was crying and scared. "Fine job, now turn around." Kyle demanded, and as he did, he felt a hard object strike the back of his head. He could hear Kyle giggle as he collapsed to the floor.

3.

He woke up to the smell of gasoline. He figured after Kyle knocked him out, he went outside and got a can of gas from whatever vehicle he was driving. He looked up and saw Kyle dousing Melissa with the gasoline and he could hear her pleas for mercy.

"Please Kyle, don't do this! I will leave him. I will come back to you; I'll do whatever you want, just please don't do this." she pleaded.

"Oh, you'll do whatever I want, huh? Tell me, in this house of God, do you renounce your love for this reprobate, this liar and charlatan, this man who is unworthy in the eyes of our Lord? Will you deny him your love, will you tell him that it is me you love and not him?" he demanded.

"Yes, yes, I will, I will do whatever you want, whatever you say," she said through her cries and sobs.

"Well looky here who is finally awake. Go on, tell him." Kyle said looking at her intently.

She turned her head toward him and looked into his eyes. He knew what she was going to say, and he knew why she was going to say it, but he also knew when he looked into Kyle's eyes it would not help them. When he did finally look into Kyles eyes, he saw nothing. He saw no soul - he saw only darkness and death. She looked at him and said, "I don't love you; I love Kyle, and Celeste is his child not yours. I never loved you, I was just lonely, and you were there." Even though he knew the words were untrue, it was still like someone had stabbed him in the heart.

"See now that wasn't hard was it? Of course, I know it's just a bunch of bullshit." Kyle said.

"What's your plan here Kyle? Kill us, take Celeste and make a run for it?" he asked trying to bide time. He had tied Melissa up but Kyle, drunk Kyle, had tied him up and did a poor job of it. if he could get him to turn away for just a moment, he could get the rest of the way free and get to him. He was just a few feet from him.

Kyle was squatting next to Melissa when he stood up. "Yeah that kind of was the plan. I got a nice little Camry parked outside and she is all gassed up." he said as he turned and pointed towards the east parking lot. He saw his chance, broke free, and made a lunging dive at Kyle like he was playing linebacker in high school again. His shoulder hit Kyle mid-section and the gun flew from Kyle's hand. He had the advantage as he wasn't drunk, but Kyle was stronger than he looked. The two fought for position and rolled a couple of times before knocking over a lit candle stand.

The floor caught on fire instantly and the fire spread rapidly towards Melissa. The alcohol that drenched Kyle's face, neck, and hands lit up instantly as did Melissa, who was covered in gas. He could hear their screams and smell burning flesh, two things that would never leave him. He moved as if to put her out, but the fire raged so intensely, he couldn't get near her. He then remembered the baby and he ran towards the office, hitting the fire alarm on his way. He picked Celeste up and ran out of the church as the screams died down.

Kyle's body was never recovered, but he was believed to be dead. After the funeral, he placed Celeste in the orphanage. He didn't want to taint her or her mother's memory by allowing people to find out she was conceived through adultery. He then accepted a position at a new church in Maple Grove and even helped a nice young couple adopt his daughter, and now he was reliving history as his sins kept coming back to haunt him.

Chapter 4.

1.

Tears welled up in his eyes as he turned the car into the orphanage parking lot. It had been a long time since he thought of the events of that night, since he and Stephanie had gotten together. She didn't cause him to forget his past, but he was able to not dwell upon it anymore. In his car he was unsure of where to begin looking.

He got out and walked into the building where he was greeted by Shareese.

"Oh my God." she said as she wrapped her arms around him into a bear hug. He swore she was going to break him in half. Shareese was a short, plump woman but he thought she was as strong as ten men. In all the years he had known her he never saw her without a smile. He worked closely with the orphanage when he was a pastor in Toledo, but he hadn't had any contact with them since he helped get Celeste adopted.

"Hello Shareese, it's been a while, and you haven't aged a day." he said manufacturing a smile. He was happy to see her, but under the circumstances, he just wanted to find the last egg and get this hunt over with. He knew if he was impolite or out of character it would raise suspicion, and one thing he was good at was avoiding suspicion. After all he had long-term relationships with two married women and had produced one child without ever raising an eyebrow.

"Oh stop, you old snake charmer. You aged but for the better. You was always a good-looking man, but now with that little salt in your hair you are looking really good." she said smiling a little devilish smile at him.

"You were always a flirt, Shareese." he said, this time smiling in earnest. "Shareese, I was wondering if I could have a look around. Maybe, check out the facility?"

"Well, I don't have time today to give you a tour, sweet thing, but you have been here a lot and not much has changed, so go ahead and look around all you want." she told him.

Just as he had turned to walk away and start looking around, he had an idea, "Shareese, is the nursery open?"

"Hmm, yes, it is. We haven't had any babies in a long while. Most of the time they go from the hospital right to the adopting parents. In fact, one of the last babies that actually stayed here was your Celeste. That poor child, losing her parents like that at so young an age. How is she doing? I mean is she still down there in that little town with you?" she asked.

"Oh yes they are doing fine. They come to church every Sunday. In fact, that is why I am here. She has started to ask about her biological parents, and in an attempt to help, I was looking for anything that might have been left here." he said trying to give a reason for his visit.

"And on Easter Sunday. You're a good man pastor Brian." she said with a smile. "Well, I can't think of anything that was left here, but go ahead and have a looksee." she said and turned back towards her office. He walked down the little hallway and if memory served him well, the nursery was on the first floor and just around the corner. He turned the corner and saw the word 'nursery' written on a plaque, screwed to the door. He opened the door and could tell right away no one had been in there in a long while. As he fumbled for the light switch, he inhaled a bit of old dust that was kicked up when he opened the door and he coughed a little bit because of it.

As he flipped the light switch on and the room lit up with a fluorescent glow, he noticed that there were no windows in that room. He wondered why he never noticed that before, but he did see a heavy steel door on the other side with the sign 'emergency exit' above it. He figured that door must have a lock on it that only allows for it to be opened from the inside. There were cribs lining the room, and four in the middle of the room. He figured at its fullest this room could house 15 babies. He remembered the one where Celeste was kept and walked right to it. She was the only baby at the time and was in the first crib in the center of the room closest to the main door. As he drew closer to the crib, he saw it right away. In the middle of the crib was a pastel purple plastic Easter egg. He couldn't figure out how the killer knew which crib Celeste had been in, but he knew that was where the egg would be.

2.

He stood there wondering what was contained in the egg this time. He wondered if it would surprise him or shock him. He wondered if he was getting used to finding disturbing things in eggs. He wondered this because he no longer dreaded opening the eggs, or what he would find in them. He wondered if this was how some police officers felt after investigating similar crimes after a while.

He opened the egg and a wet bloody round object fell out and landed in the crib. As he stared into the crib, he saw exactly what it was. One of Stephanie's green eyes was looking back at him. The last time they were together, he remembered he told her that he loved her eyes and he loved looking into them. Was the killer there? Did he hear us? And, if so, how?

"HOLY JESUS!" he heard her scream and wheeled around to see Shareese standing in the door and looking at the eyeball in the crib. "OH MY, MY GOD WHAT IS THAT?" she asked, "Is that, is that an eye?" he quickly moved to her and guided her out of the room.

"Shh, shh. Shareese, Shareese look at me." he said, and she did.

"What is going on?" she asked with a look of fear, desperation, and confusion on her face.

"I can't tell you that. Please you have to trust me." he said.

"Trust you? I haven't seen you in 8 years or better and when I do, I find you in the nursery with a human eye. Oh no, no what I need to do is call the police." she pronounced as poh-leese.

"You can't call the police Shareese. If you do, he will kill her." he said a little more sternly than he intended. It was the first time he had said anything about this out loud to anyone. The gravity of it hit him and it took all his strength to not break down completely. If it wasn't for Celeste, he would have.

"Who is going to kill who?" she asked.

"I don't know, but I know that someone has Celeste and her family, and if I tell anyone or call the police, they will all die. I'm pretty sure that eye belonged to Celeste's mom Stephanie, along with the other parts I found." he wanted to stop talking but he couldn't. It was all flowing out of him now.

"Tell me what's going on Sugar, maybe I can help?" she said, and he did. He told her everything from the first affair, to him being Celeste's biological father, to the current affair with Celeste's adopted mother and all about the maniacal Easter egg hunt he had been on all day. He told her everything.

"So you see, you can't call the cops. At least not yet. I have about an hour to figure out the last clue. Can you give me that? Can you give me an hour?" he begged.

"Yeah honey, I can. What is the last clue?" she asked.

"I don't know, I haven't read it yet." he replied. He turned and walked back into the room and picked up the egg where it fell when she startled him. She was right behind him and as curious as he was. When he unfurled the piece of paper, he read the clue aloud. "Clue 6: Hebrews Chapter 13 verse 4: Marriage should be honored by all, and the marriage bed kept pure, for God will judge the adulterer and all the sexually immoral. Come to where this all began so we can finish it. Come alone preacher, so we can close the circle once and for all."

"You understand it don't ya? You know who it is?" she asked but she knew the truth, she could see it on his face.

"Yes, I have to go to my old church. I have to face him." he said coldly.

"If he was going to face you anyways why go through all of this?" she asked.

"To punish me, to wear me down so I will be easier to deal with when we meet." he said. "I have to go. Please remember one hour, then you can call whomever you want. Ok?" he said

"Ok, 1 hour." she said holding up her right index finger to emphasize the one.

3.

He went to the car, deposited the egg with the eyeball in it inside the plastic bag and gave it to Shareese.

"After you call the cops, give them this bag and tell them everything you know." he told her.

"You don't think you're coming back, do you?" she asked.

"No. I think Stephanie is dead and I hope I can save Celeste and Greg. If I have to give my life for that, then so be it. I will gladly do so. Plus, I think he plans on killing me quickly. For him it's been 11 years, so I am positive he wants this over." he said, and she gave him another bear hug.

"You have sinned, but by God haven't we all. Repent your sins, beg for God's forgiveness before you go into that church. Become the man we all know you can be." she told him. He nodded his head, got into his car and drove away, headed for his old church.

4.

It was a little past 4 p.m. when he arrived at his old church, most of the old building had burnt to the ground and had to be rebuilt, but it was done exactly as it was when he was the pastor. He parked in his old parking spot. He didn't wonder if the church was unlocked, he knew it would be. He also knew that he was going right to the sanctuary. That was where he would find all of them, waiting for him.

He picked up the small six-shot revolver from the seat beside him. He made sure not to raise it above dash in case he was being watched.

Shareese had pulled it out of her purse and given it to him before he gave her the bag of plastic eggs. She said she carried it for protection - she did live alone in Toledo after all. He opened the cylinder and saw that every chamber was filled. He placed the gun in his waist band at the small of his back, like he had seen people do in many movies. He untucked his shirt to try and hide the gun. He got out of his car and headed toward the church.

He grabbed the handle of the church door and froze. All day he had lived in fear, but this fear froze him in place. This fear brought out a side in him he didn't like. This fear made him think about if they were all dead already, and by opening the door he was sealing his own fate. This fear made him think he should turn around, get back in his car and just drive away. He steeled himself and opened the door hard and quick. Part of him expected it to be locked, no; *hoped* it would be locked, but it swung open freely and he stepped inside.

As he walked into the large room where services were held, probably as recently as this morning, he saw two people sitting in chairs in the sanctuary. He rushed towards them and saw that they were tied with duct tape to the chairs. Each hand and each foot was taped to the chair individually. They had tape around their legs, abdomen and chest. Their mouths and eyes were also taped shut. They were sitting on each side of the entrance; Greg was to his right and Celeste was to his left. He went through the little gate that separated the sanctuary from the nave and instantly turned left to free Celeste first.

"Good evening preacher." the man said. He had a deep voice and it sounded like he had gravel in his throat when he spoke. "Now how did I know you would go to the girl first? I guess you did always have a thing for the ladies, am I right Greg?" he said. Pastor Brian stopped, lowered his head and turned towards the voice. Greg didn't even make a sound. "Don't worry preacher. I didn't tell your dirty little secret to any of them. Your sins are for you to tell, to confess."

"Kyle," he said. "I thought you were dead."

"Well I was dead preacher, and then I was resurrected just like our Lord and savior Jesus Christ." he said stepping into the light for the first time. Pastor Brian could see that the man before him, the man that was once Kyle Gardner, was disfigured beyond recognition. His face, neck, and hands were scarred and looked like something out of a horror movie. He held a gun in his right hand and leaned on a cane with his left. The man noticed Brian looking at him with horror and disgust. "Not as pretty as I once was, am I preacher? You made sure of that didn't ya? But then again, I never was as pretty as you were. Was that how you stole her, with your pretty boy looks and fancy words? Did you corrupt her with fancy talk and pretty boy eyes?"

"She was lonely. I was lonely. We just came together. It wasn't planned. You know this, she told you all this. She told me what she said to you." he said.

"Oh, yeah she told me. I wonder if that's what happened with this new girl, preacher. Was she lonely? Greg, was your wife lonely?" This time Greg did make a noise. "That's right, the preacher man here has been tending to your wife's every need and desire. He was spreading his seed to her as he did my wife. Go forth and multiply, sayeth the Lord." he said.

"Why are you doing this? Why are you hurting innocent people? You want to hurt me? Fine. I'm not innocent, but let them go." he said

"I came to find you about a year ago preacher. I was hell-bent on ending my life and I wanted you to know it. I wanted you to suffer with the thought of me killing myself in front of you. I wanted you to have to live with not one, but two ruined lives and dead souls on your conscience. I sat there on a bench and watched as your flock left service, and then I saw that young girl there and I thought, oh my God that is the spitting image of my Melissa. I saw her leave with Greg and Stephanie. I saw the way you and Stephanie looked at each other and I just knew, but I had to be sure. So, I did some research, checked the local libraries and broke into the church and your files. And then I broke into their home and checked their files. I followed you both, put hidden video recording devices in the areas you frequented. It's amazing what you can get online today, it really is. I learned the truth, and now it's time preacher. It's time to confess your sins, it's time to tell the truth." he said pointing the gun at Celeste.

"Whoa, whoa, just stop. Fine I will tell them everything, then you will allow them to leave right?" he begged.

"Oh preacher, let's just say I won't kill them right away. I will give you the opportunity to convince me to let them live." he said. "And if you can't, as long as you do confess, I promise to kill them quickly. They won't suffer like my Melissa or Stephanie did, and suffer she did."

"Where is Stephanie?" Brian asks finally, not wanting to know the truth.

"She died for her sins preacher, and she died horribly as you already know. But I will say this; she was one tough woman and she loved you very much. Now confess, confess to these good people right here." he said, using the gun to gesture towards them.

"Ok, ok." he said taking a deep breath and turning towards the man taped to a chair. "Greg," he pauses, swallows, and breathes. "Stephanie and I have been having an affair for well over a year now. We-- we were in love with each other and had plans to be together soon. Permanently. She was going to leave you." he said. He could hear Greg make noises, angry noises, and he could hear him start to cry.

"That's a good start preacher, but I wonder, was it the woman or the kid you really wanted? You're not done." he ordered.

"Celeste, years ago I fell in love with another woman, and she was married as well. We had an affair for years." he paused again. "I had gotten her pregnant. For almost a year we allowed her husband to believe that the child was his. That was one of the cruelest things I have ever done in my life. The other truly cruel thing I have done, was never tell that girl that I am her father. Celeste, you were that child. I am your father." he said. Greg made more sounds and this time Celeste joined him.

"Go on, preacher. Finish it! Finish your tale of sin and woe." Kyle said.

"I am the reason you're all in this. It was this man's wife whom I impregnated, and it was my sins that led us to this moment. It was my sins that caused him to do the things he has done. I pray for God's forgiveness but it's your forgiveness I need Celeste, yours as well Greg, and even yours Kyle." he said slowly turning towards the burnt man. The part he feared was over, and now he wanted to make the burnt man look away long enough so he could pull out his gun and end this. It was time to end this. It was time for him to put on a show.

"My forgiveness will never be yours preacher." Kyle said.

"But it was not my sin alone," Brian continued, "for he who brought us to this moment has sin of his own, he has sinned in the eyes of the Lord." he said turning sideways to see the man, positioning himself for a good shot.

"No sir, no I have not, I have been reborn without sin. I do God's true work. I root out the sinner and make them repent in front of God and the ones he did wrong. I am free of sin". he said raising his hands and spreading his arms out wide. When he did this, Brian seized upon his opportunity. He pulled the gun from behind his back, aimed, and fired. The burnt man fell backwards and lay motionless.

Brian quickly went to Celeste and untied her and the two of them proceeded to untie her adoptive father.

"Is everything you said true?" she asked, and he nodded. After Greg was untied, he stood up and punched the pastor in the mouth.

"We will settle this further when we get home, but I need to get MY daughter out of here." Greg said. Brian laid there for a moment and said nothing. He knew he deserved this and more, and he agreed they needed to get Celeste out of there.

They left the nave through the open double doors and headed towards the front doors. Celeste and Greg went through the front set of glass doors, when they heard a single gunshot. They turned and saw Pastor Brian stop and fall to his knees before falling over dead with a bullet hole in his back. They saw the burnt man lying on the floor with his gun raised and a bloody smile on his face. The burnt man then turned the gun towards himself, placed the barrel against his temple and squeezed the trigger.

6.

Greg and Celeste rushed out of the last set of glass doors into the fresh evening air. They could hear the sirens in the background getting closer and they knew where they were headed. Greg also knew that Celeste saw everything, that she saw that man kill himself, that she saw his brains exit his head and splatter against the wooden door. He wanted to protect her, and he had failed. He loved his daughter and he also knew that she would need therapy. Hell they both would, but he knew he loved her as much now as the day he first saw her and that he would always be there for her.

"You ok, Dad?" she asked, and then he knew she would be alright.

The End.

Fourth of July

American Hero?

Chapter 1.

1.

"Hey, Hello, there buddy. How ya feeling?"

"George? Where am I?"

"Well, that's a good question."

"Whoa, why are my hands tied? What's going on? George?!"

"Well I can't have you flailing around when the cutting starts, now can I? You might injure yourself."

"Cutting? Why, why would there be cutting?"

"Well I can't imagine you being fully honest with me when the questioning begins."

"Questioning? What are you going on about, George?"

"Saaid, do you think that I believe it was merely coincidence that you moved in next to me, just mere months after the trade centers were destroyed? I know there is another attack coming. What I don't know is when or where, and you will tell me that."

"George, I don't know!"

"Shh, let's not start off with lies already."

"George, please. Listen, I really don't know what you're talking about. Why would I?"

"This is to be expected, I suppose. Of course, you're scared, why wouldn't you be. Look, this can be over quick, or it can last a long time. It's your choice. Tell me what I need to know, and it will end quickly, I promise."

"I don't know anything George. If I did, I would tell you. You don't have to hurt me. Just let me go and we can chalk it up to a prank."

"A prank? A prank!? I AM TRYING TO SAVE LIVES AND YOU THINK THIS IS A FUCKING PRANK!?... No Saaid, this is not a prank. This is me doing whatever it takes to prevent another terrorist attack on this country. To prevent more innocent deaths."

"I swear I don't know anything; Please George don't do this. I am not a terrorist and I don't want to hurt anyone. Please, please don't do this."

"I wish I didn't have to do this Saaid I really do, but I have no choice. Before we begin though, let me wish you a happy Fourth of July."

Chapter 2.

1.

George walked away and Saaid started to realize the gravity of the situation he was in. He realized he was naked and strapped to a metal table. Both hands and feet were strapped individually, with another strap across his abdomen and one across his chest. His head however was not strapped down, and he looked around for the first time since he woke up. He looked like he was in a run down, abandoned factory. He couldn't tell what time of day it was since there were no windows to look out of, but he felt it was probably still early in the day. He tried to remember how he got here.

2.

BZZZZ BZZZZ BZZZZ.

He reached over and shut his alarm off. *4 a.m. already,* he thought as he sat up. He was never the type to hit the snooze button. He felt the snooze button was made for those who wished to sleep their life away. He preferred to attack life, to make the most of it, so he swung his legs over the bed, put his feet in his slippers that awaited him and headed downstairs to start his morning ritual.

First thing he did was turn on some classical music. He believed music in the morning helped wake up the soul. He would then walk to the kitchen to turn on the coffee machine. He then headed back upstairs to take his shower and get ready for the day ahead. Afterwards he would stand there in his three-piece suit and admire himself in the mirror. He was actually looking to make sure everything was perfect. His father always told him people expect what they see, and he wanted them to see success in him.

He headed downstairs for his morning bowl of fruit and English muffin with cream cheese. As he ate his breakfast, he would read the newspaper. Most people his age liked to get the news from social media or the internet, he however preferred to hold the paper in his hands. He loved the smell of it, the feel of it, and the permanence of it. After breakfast he loaded his few dishes into the dishwasher and made sure everything was tidy. He then exited the kitchen into his garage and hit the button on his key fob to start the car, pressing the button on the wall to open the garage. Once settled in his $100,000 Lexus, he checked his mirrors and in it he saw something strange. He swore he saw his neighbor George in his back seat.

3.

George knew all the tricks to this house. He had been in it so many times back when The Hunter's owned it. Scott Hunter was probably George's best friend. They had gone to college together, their wives were best friends, they spent every 4th of July together (until this one that is), and both worked in the World Trade Center. Scott had bought his house a couple of years before George, and was in fact the reason George bought the one next door. Scott was at work that fateful day on September 11th and shortly after Scott's wife, Miriam, sold the house to a foreigner and moved back to Philadelphia where her parents were.

Now, George was laying in the backseat of a very expensive Lexus, awaiting the arrival of that foreigner. He knew something was off the minute he met Saaid a few months back, shortly after he moved in. He wondered how a foreigner was able to buy such an expensive house. He watched as movers showed up and realized they were all brown like him. He then began to suspect that maybe a terrorist had moved in next door.

Chapter 3.

1.

"Alright one last chance. I beg you Saaid, please tell me the plan. I don't want to do this, so please don't make me."

"if you don't want to do this, then don't. It's your choice."

"I wish it was, but we both know it's not. I must protect the people and country I care about. So, tell me the plan and this all goes away."

"Listen to me George. There is no plan. I am not what you think I am."

"I want you to know I did research on this and looked it up on the internet, so I have a good grasp on what I'm about to do and all you have to do to stop me is tell me the truth."

"I am telling you the truth. I swear it."

"Ok, well to start I am going to take this scalpel and cut just deep enough on your leg here to get under the skin, and then I am going to pull that skin back and cut it away from the muscle."

"What? No wait, aaaagghhhhhh."

"That sounded like it really hurt. Messier than I thought it would be. Let me clean it up a bit."

"AAAagghhhhhh."

"Oops, that was the saltwater. Oh well, no use crying over spilt saltwater now is there. Now Saaid, where would you like me to cut next huh? Speak up. Or how about you just tell me the truth?"

"I DON'T KNOW ANYTHING YOU DOLT!"

"Well now name calling is uncalled for; I am just doing what I have to Saaid. I think you of all people should be able to understand that. So, where next? How about the chest?"

"Aaaaaggghhhhhh, aaaaggghhhhhh!"

"That nipple was kind of hard to get off there. Are you ready to talk yet?"

"Go fuck yourself, George."

"Well, I guess we're going to continue then."

Chapter 4.

1.

"What a beautiful day." George thought when he walked out of his front door that morning. He also thought what a shame it was to waste the morning cooped up in an office. He got into his car and backed out of his driveway. He then turned right at the stop sign instead of left and called his secretary.

"Schultz Export and Import, George McCall's office. How may I help you?" the female voice on the other end said.

"Jeanine this is George. What does my calendar look like this morning?"

She knew this meant he wanted to skip out that morning and play golf. She knew when he called about his calendar what he really wanted. She also hated when he called because that meant if he had any meetings or clients scheduled that day, she would have to reschedule them, and she hated to reschedule. Plus, if she had called in to say she would be late so she could play golf, she would have been fired on the spot. "Well sir, you're actually all cleared up this morning." Which, for a change, was not a lie.

"Good, I will be in late, a beautiful day like today should be spent on the greens and not inside. I will see you around lunch. If you need me, I will have my cell on, ok?"

"Ok sir, see you then. Have fun and hope you have a good game." This time she did lie, she hoped he had a bad game and gave him a nasty look he would never see. She wanted to just quit and walk out right then and there, but the two little ones that were in school needed her to keep her job a little while longer.

2.

As he reached the green of hole one, he had a clear view of the city and the two towers. He could see the south tower where his office was located. He loved this view and spent many hours just staring out towards the golf course wishing he was there. Today he was. He loved this course and since he brought potential clients there and subsequently lost to them, the company paid for his membership.

As he lined up his shot, he heard a loud crash and looked up towards the city. He could see smoke coming from the north tower and wondered what had happened. He and his caddy were the only ones out there that morning and they watched as a plane struck the south tower. He felt the fear grow inside of him. He thought of Scott and Jeanine and all the people he had worked with for the last 20 plus years. He watched as both towers collapsed, and a giant cloud of dust rose into the sky and spread throughout the city. He could feel that fear growing inside him, but something else was growing in him as well. It was a feeling that was strange to him, he had felt it before as a child and again as a young man, but it had been a very long time. He began to recognize it as guilt.

The ringing of his cell phone brought him out of his trance. As he reached for it, he hoped it was Scott or maybe Jeanine calling to let him know they were alright. He looked at the screen prior to answering it and read the word HOME. His heart fell a little. He answered it, "Amy it's ok, I'm ok. I wasn't at the office I was at the course.... Yes, I decided last minute to go golfing.... Yes, I am on my way home now.... Do they know what happened? Well what does the news say? Alright, alright I will be home in a minute." After he hung up, he hurried to his car leaving his clubs with the caddy and not changing out of his golfing clothes and shoes. He drove home as quickly as he could. Once home he and his wife sat in front of the television and watched as the horrors of terrorism played out in front of them.

Over the next few months he attended more funerals than he could count. Funerals of friends and co-workers he had known for most of the later part of his life. He struggled trying to find a new job at his age that would afford him the lifestyle he and his family had become accustomed to. In fact, he had trouble finding any job. They were blowing through their savings and at that rate it would be gone within a year, and his retirement not long after. He still had the kid's college fund if he needed but he hoped not to need that. A little while later Miriam Hunter sold the house, and Saaid moved in.

3.

He heard the door leading to the house open and felt the car start. He then heard the garage door begin its upward track. He took the rag and put it over the bottle opening. Tipping the bottle and dousing the rag with chloroform, he had seen this done many times in movies and hoped they didn't lie about its effects. He also hoped Saaid didn't see him in the back seat before he had a chance to act.

He heard the door open and felt the driver's side seat as Saaid sat down. He waited a few seconds and then sat up. He saw Saaid's eyes grow wide in confusion in the rearview mirror and he placed the wet cloth over Saaid's mouth and nose. He could feel Saaid struggle, and then he could feel when Saaid lost consciousness.

Chapter 5.

1.

"Man, you scream. Guess I should have got those earplugs after all."

"G-go f-fuck y-yourself eorge."

" I will give you this; you are one tough son of a bitch. I mean there almost isn't any skin left to remove and not only do you still have a voice, but you're still not telling me what I need to know. See this gun? All I got to do is put it to your head and squeeze the trigger and all of this, all of this pain goes away. If you don't want that to happen, all you have to do is tell me what I need to know. Tell me about the next attack, please?"

"I-I D-Don know-w any-anything. Y-You b-bloody American m-moron."

"Alright suit yourself, but I will have to change tactics. Let me clean you up a bit. Now stay still because this will hurt, saltwater is a bitch on open wounds."

""Aaaaaggghhhhhh, aaaaggghhhhhh, aaaaggghhhhhh, aaaaggghhhhhh, aaaaggghhhhhh, aaaaggghhhhhh!"

"Oh, quit ya big baby, that wasn't so bad. A bit over dramatic don't ya think? Now comes the part where I start cutting stuff off and out of ya. You ever see the movie Braveheart? Remember at the end, when Mel Gibson was strapped to a table much like this one and they yanked his guts out? Well, they didn't show that, but they did have this midget man do a little reenactment before, so the audience knew what was happening off screen. Well that's the next step, and once I start that there is no turning back, no recovering from that, just a long painful death. So, anything to say before I start? .... No, ok then."

"Alright, a-alright, I-I will t-talk. c-come c-closer.... hahaha."

"YOU'RE GOING TO SPIT IN MY EYE WITH YOUR DISGUSTING, DISEASE RIDDEN, UNCLEAN, UNHOLY,

FILTH. YOU SICK SON OF A BITCH! I HAVE BEEN NOTHING BUT RESPECTFUL TO YOU AND YOUR GODLESS KIND BECAUSE OF THE CIRCUMSTANCE! THE CIRCUMSTANCE YOU FORCED ME TO PUT YOU IN. YOU AND THE F.B.I. ARE TO BLAME FOR THIS! Yeah, that's right I called them. I had you investigated, and apparently, they weren't smart enough to catch on to what you are, but I did. Every time I called them back, they kept giving me the run around up to the point of agent dipshit getting on the phone and saying they are still investigating but haven't found anything yet. Well I told Agent Gardner dipshit that I knew you were a terrorist and that I was going to get proof. So you see? You and agent dipshit forced my hand, you forced me to use unconventional means to obtain information that would save lives. THIS IS ALL YOUR DAMN FAULT!"

"Aaaaaggghhhhhh, aaaaggghhhhhh!"

"Damn, see what you made me do. Oh well, just gonna have to finish cutting you open and start the disembowelment."

Chapter 6.

1.

They pulled up to the abandoned warehouse silently. There were 5 cars in total, each with 2 officers. He didn't want to spook him, so the order for no lights and sirens had been given. He hoped to surprise him and not give the perp a chance to escape or kill his vic.

He became suspicious of Mr. George McCall when he said he would do what he needed to get proof that his new neighbor was a terrorist. Since 9/11, his office alone had received more people calling in to report a supposed terrorist than in the whole 10 years he had been at the New Jersey office. They tried to investigate as many calls as they could, but there was no way they could investigate them all, and so he gave Mr. McCall the standard "we are investigating" line, but he just wouldn't have it. He then heard over the wire that a Mr. Saaid Abdalla did not report for work and no one could seem to get ahold of him. He knew something was wrong. He recognized the name and connected it to McCall and the conversation they had the other day. He drove over to the Abdalla house and saw the garage door wide open. He then ran Abdallah through the system for the first time. He was an Indian (not the cowboys and Indians kind, he thought to himself) Muslim from London, the son of a wealthy man and was in the states to start a new restaurant in New York City. There were other things, things that had he looked into them he might have actually suspected him as a radical Muslim and potential terrorist. Nothing concrete, just a few associations, but he should have investigated, and he knew it. He also saw the type of vehicle that Abdallah owned. A Lexus, an expensive Lexus, no doubt bought by daddy he thought. He knew the car was gone and called to see if it was low jacked. It was. They found it at an abandoned warehouse about 5 miles outside of the city. He called his partner and then they rendezvoused with a few locals to go to the warehouse.

He knew Abdallah had been missing for hours and didn't want to think of the state he was in.

They checked the doors and all, but none were locked. They quietly entered and started to search the place looking for McCall and Abdallah. As they neared the center of the factory, Agent Gardner saw McCall covered in blood and leaning over an obviously dead Saaid Abdallah. He pointed his gun at McCall and stepped out shouting "FREEZE, F.B.I. PUT YOUR HANDS UP AND STEP AWAY.".

"He is about to tell me about the next attack, just give me a few more minutes. Please."

"Step away from the body Mr. McCall." Gardner said as he saw the gun that was in McCall's hand. "And put down the gun. Now!"

"Just a little longer please!" McCall said raising his hands to expound, "I just nee" he was cut off as the sound of gunfire came from behind Gardner. Two of the officers who had their guns drawn and aimed on McCall opened fire when they saw the gun raised in his hand. McCall fell back on to the floor. He didn't move. McCall was shot 4 times, center mass and was most likely dead before he hit the floor.

"Damn it!" Gardner said.

2.

Hours after they arrived, Gardner and his partner Agent Smith - whom Gardner loved to razz about his name - talked as the coroner and CSI did their job.

"So, do you think he was a terrorist?" Smith asked.

"I don't know. Maybe, but now we may never now. What I do know is if this keeps happening" he said gesturing towards the warehouse, "If we keep acting out with hate toward anyone who we see as different, then they win."

"Who wins?" Smith asks.

"The Terrorists." Gardner replied heavy hearted.

The End.

Halloween

The Vengeance of Cassidy Clay

Sit right there and I will tell you a tale,
One as old as time and scary as hell.
About a midnight rider out on the loose,
Be careful, or you might end up in his noose.
This is the tale of Cassidy Clay,
An evil man is most every way.
Oh, how he loved to hunt down a runaway slave,
Was supposed to bring 'em back but preferred 'em in
their grave.
"Hang 'em all one by one" they heard him say,
"Stretch their necks and watch 'em sway".
If Cassidy Clay had you, there is one fact,
Black or white you would never come back.
He was protected by the law,
Until the murder of Miss Sarah Shaw.
Cassidy Clay was already hated by all,
But her death was the start of his downfall.

A preacher's daughter in a small southern town,
Sarah Shaw was loved all around.
No one loved her more,
Than the man she could not ignore.

Jesse Whitman was born a slave y'all,
Son of the white man who owned them all.
He wasn't treated as a slave,
He bound around town, brazen and brave.

Slave according to the law,
But in Ellersville, slaves they were not at all.
His father and mother lived as husband and wife,
Treated as a rich man's son all his life.
When Jesse first saw Sarah, it was love at first sight,
When she saw him, her heart started to glow bright.

For 6 months they snuck around,
Meeting in a clearing just outside of town.
Wanting to keep this love they had begun,
Not wanting to share with the world what they had
become.
All was good until that fateful day,
When everything changed and the good died away.
As she awaited her love on the late October date,
But Jessie was running very late.
She heard someone who could not stay put,
Out of the woods came a runaway slave on foot.
She asked him his name and why he was running,
He called himself Mathias and he asked for one thing.
A place to hide since he was a runaway,
He said a man was after him named Cassidy Clay.
As she tried to show him a place to lay low,
Clay appeared and as he got closer, he seemed to grow.
He looked them over for a long while,
"Two for one" he said with a smile.
He hung them both from the large oak tree next to a
red spruce,
He hung them high from a freshly fastened noose.
When Jessie arrived, he saw a man riding away,
His love dangling and starting to sway.
In anger and grief, he gave chase,
Jessie was fast but this was not a race.
Clay turned on him with speed and skill,

Gun in hand he shot him at will.
Clay then rode into town to tell the sheriff what he had done,
And claim the bounty that he had won.
But instead of money he was given chains,
He was protected by law he tried to explain.
In this town murder he did commit,
And they would find a justice that would fit.
On Halloween night they gathered around,
And took Clay to the clearing just outside of town.
And on the large oak next to a red spruce,
They hung him high with his own noose.
I wish I could tell you my friends,
I wish I could say this is where the story ends.
In a final breath he spoke one last time,
He screamed to the night "Vengeance will be mine".
Over the course of the next few years,
Members of that lynch mob would disappear.
They would be found in those woods you see,
Hung by the neck and swaying in the breeze.

To this very day on Halloween night,
You can find Clay on his vengeful plight.
Just last fall as Halloween drew near,
Some brave young people showed no fear.
As they trekked into his woods for a Halloween treat,
It was Clay they were hoping to meet.
As night fell, they started to wander about,
His name they began to shout.
On the wind they could hear his ghostly laugh,
They pulled out their phones hoping for a photograph.
Brad, the leader of the pack, was the first to go,
A braver young man you would never know.
As the group neared that special place,

Brad disappeared without a trace.
No one had seen him vanish from sight,
Their search turned towards him that night.
As they feared Brad was lost,
It was Clay whose path they crossed.
Shelley was the next to go,
She was gone before the rest could know.
As the rope slid around her throat,
Ghostly hands tightened it and she began to choke.
Into the trees he pulled her away,
They wouldn't find her body till the following day.
Another victim Cassidy had claimed,
Swaying in the breeze to the shouts of her name.
Feeling her fate was sealed and she was gone,
The last two ran and prayed for dawn.
Only one would escape his grasp,
I made it to town before I collapsed.
My other friend they never found,
To those woods she is still bound.

Cassidy still the haunts those woods to this very day,
So come Halloween do yourself a favor and stay away.
If you go in there with friend or by yourself,
Cassidy will send you to hell along with everyone else.

The End.

Thanksgiving

The Feast

Chapter 1

1.

Thursday, November 21. Thanksgiving Day.

"Hey, check the GPS?"

"Ok, well it's not saying anything new... because It has no signal."

"Great. Can you hear me now? Apparently not." she laughs when he says this. He can always make her laugh. "Well I'm pretty sure we are on this road for a while, so hopefully we reconnect before we have any turns."

She looks at him and smiles. She knows he didn't really want to go on this trip, it's her parents after all, and they don't get along well. They usually do Thanksgiving at his parents who only live 45 minutes away versus hers who are 4 hours away, and the fastest way is back roads through the winding hills. She doesn't need the GPS, she has travelled this way many times on her return trips from college where they met, but he likes using it and it makes him feel comfortable.

She appreciates what he is doing. Her parents usually come see them on Christmas Day, but they are going on a cruise this year, so they switched the holiday trips to accommodate them. She knows it upset him a little, but not enough to even make a little stink about it. She turns to look at their son, sleeping in his car seat. He is 4 years old, and in her eyes, he is perfect.

2.

He jokes to make himself feel more comfortable. It's raining hard and he has rarely travelled these roads. That makes him a bit nervous. He doesn't like driving through unknown country, or backwoods country as his dad called. He is a city boy, born and bred, and prefers to stay in cities. He never had much care for the "country life", or its backwoods people, but he loves his wife and to make her happy he would drive through the Ponderosa itself. Not to mention that they are on their way to her parent's house.

Her parent's house, a joy to be had for sure. He does not like them, not one bit. It still amazes him how those two created and raised this amazing woman that he was lucky to be married to. Her mom acts all dim-witted to throw people off, but in reality, she is very perceptive. She drinks vodka like most people drink water, probably to numb the realization of the man she married. She is old school and won't leave him for anything.

Her father, well that's another story. He was rich by all accounts shortly after college and loves to rub that in his face. The pretentious ass is either too absorbed in his own world to notice his wife's alcohol usage or flat out just doesn't care. He doesn't hit her, never has, as that might show he had a heart.

He tries not to hold on to his dislike of them but just can't help it. It's been there since their first meeting. He doesn't think she truly likes them much either, but she does love them and since they are getting older, they won't be around much longer. Then they are God's problem, he thinks.

As he thinks this, he sees her look into the back seat out of the corner of his eye. He takes his eyes off the road for that second to look at her looking at their son. When he looks back, he sees something in the road. He reacts but too late. The car hits the object on the driver's side front corner panel before the mid-size SUV launches off the road and bashes dead on against a tree.

Chapter 2

1.

Ding, ding, ding.

As her eyes slowly open, she can hear a ringing in her head. *Ding, ding, ding.* Her head hurts, she wonders what happened. *Ding, ding, ding.* As her head clears, she realizes what that sound is. It is the sound the car makes when a door is left open. *Ding, ding, ding.* She fully opens her eyes and realizes quickly what happened. They were in an accident. *Ding, ding, ding.* She sits up and sees the inflated air bag before her, she struggles against it trying to look behind her to check on Mikey. He is only four after all. *Ding, ding, ding.* Her hands find a pen and she stabs the airbag. It makes a loud sound, like a balloon popping, and lets the air out. *Ding, ding, ding.* The sound continues almost as if it is mocking her. *Ding, ding, ding.* As the air lets out of the airbag, she turns her eyes towards the back seat. *Ding, ding, ding.* As the sound fills the air, fear fills her body. *Ding, ding, ding.* She looks in horror at the empty car seat that held her son, that was supposed to protect him in an event such as this. *Ding, ding, ding.* Her first thought was that he was somehow thrown from the car. *ding, ding, ding.*

"John." she says. "John!" she screams when he didn't respond the first time. She hopes he is ok. She is sure he is; she is after all. "John, Michael is missing!"

2.

"John!" he hears her scream but barely. He feels the air bag inflated against his face. "Aren't these things supposed to deflate after a few minutes?" he thinks. He needs to check on that and if it is, he is calling the dealership first thing Monday morning and letting them have it.

"John, Michael is missing!" he hears her this time, clearly. His head clears, it hurts, but it's clear. He struggles against the air bag until he hears a loud pop and the bag deflates instantly. He sees her, she has a pen in her hand, and the look of pure fear on her face. He instantly checks the back seat, thinking maybe he is sitting on the floor and she missed him, hoping he is but he is not. Now he hears it. *Ding, ding, ding.* This noise has become the soundtrack to their worst fears. *Ding, ding, ding.* Now that he hears it, he cannot unhear it. *Ding, ding, ding.* He unbuckles his belt and forces his door open. It fights against him, but he eventually gets it open enough to squeeze out. *Ding, ding, ding.* He sees her doing the same. Her door is not as crumpled as his and she has an easier time. As he stands his head starts to swoon, but he gathers his balance and uses the vehicle to steady himself as he rushes around the rear end. As he comes to the passenger side, he sees her standing there looking towards the woods. *Ding, ding, ding.*

She told him the back door was already open. Michael has learned how to unbuckle himself from the seat a while ago, but "how did he open the door? The child locks were on, weren't they?" she wonders to herself.

He suddenly remembers last Wednesday night. He had used her SUV to go to work because his car was getting some maintenance done. After work him and a few people from the office went out for a few drinks as they do for every holiday break. He remembers he gave some of them a ride home as they drank too much to drive themselves. He undid the child locks because he didn't want to get out and open the door for them, after all he wasn't their chauffeur. Imagining the hazing he would have gotten on Monday morning, so he undid the child locks and forgot to reset them. This is his fault he thinks, his fault. *Ding, Ding, Ding.*

Chapter 3

1.

When he wakes, his neck and head hurt. He sees his parents. They look like they are sleeping on big white pillows. In fact, there are pillows all around him. The car is stopped so he unbuckles his seat. He is not allowed to unbuckle his seat when they are moving, but when they stop, he is.

He gets down and leans between the two front seats. "Mommy, mommy," he tries to wake her, but she doesn't move. He turns to look at his dad and calls to him but to no avail. He feels scared. He decides to go for help and tries to open his door. It's usually locked and won't open, but this time the door swings open when he pulls the handle and pushes on it.

Climbing down from the car, he sees where the car hit the tree. "Ouchy car. When mommy wakes up, she will get a band-aid for your hurt." he tells the inanimate object. He decides to head into the woods to find help. He knows not to go too far bur doesn't know how far is too far.

He walks what feels like forever. He stops and looks around; everything looks the same. He decides to head back to the car, to his parents, but he doesn't know which way that is. He starts to walk back the way he came but then thinks he sees a familiar tree and heads that way. After a while, a long while, he decides to sit down next to a tree. He starts to be truly scared for the first time. Scared, tired, and hungry. He starts to cry. He wonders if his parents are all right. He wonders if he will ever see them again. He cries harder, louder.

"Hello?" he hears someone and looks around wiping the tears from his eyes. He thinks maybe it's his mommy or daddy. "Mommy, Daddy!" he cries out, hoping.

2.

As the two men are walking through the woods, they hear what sounds like a child crying. The older of the two looks at the younger in questioning surprise and calls out "Hello?".

"Mommy, Daddy!" he hears back, and the two men start heading in the direction of the voice. As they pass two large oak trees, they see him; a small child sitting on the ground and leaning against one of the trees. The older man kneels and looks at the boy's face. He can see the soft round cheeks red and stained with tears, he can see the fear in the boy's big blue eyes. "Well, where did you come from?" he asks the child.

"I dunno." the boy says.

"Ok, what do you know? Let's start with your name?" he says this in a soft voice to help put the child at ease.

"Michael, but I'm not supposed to", which comes out as *pose to*, "talk to strangers, but I can't find my mommy and daddy," he starts crying again, "and I'm cold, hungry and the car is hurt, and they didn't wake up! Why didn't they wake up?"

"Shh, shh it's okay. My name is Randy, and this is my little brother Adam. Now we're not strangers anymore, and we are gonna help you find your parents, okay?" he says and the little boy nods and even smiles a bit. Randy smiles back as he picks the boy up.

As his new friend Randy lifts him into the air easily like his daddy does, he asks Randy "Where are we going?"

"Well buddy, we are going to take you back to our place. See our family comes up here every year for Thanksgiving and our mom can take care of you while we look for your parents."

"I'm hungry, can I have a snack?" he thinks about this then adds "please?"

"Oh, I'm sure we can find something for you to eat. Aren't you a polite young man."

"Mommy always says you gotta have good manners."

"Yes, you do. She is right about that."

3.

They walk in silence until they come into the clearing.
Michael's eyes get big when he sees the large green
house. He can see a large wooden deck on the back of
the house with two doors next to each other at the
center of the deck. There is a swing on one side big
enough for a couple of large people to sit on, he thinks,
and a bunch of little table and chairs all around it. On
the other side he sees a grill, but it's got a cover on it.
He knows what this is because his dad has one and they
cook on it when it's nice outside. When they open one
of the doors to enter, he can smell all the delicious
smells coming from inside and hears a large group of
people talking and laughing.

"Well, who you got there Randy?" Michael hears and
turns around to see an older woman, who reminds him
of his gramma Suzy - his daddy's mom - not his gramma
Bev who is skinny and always has a drink in her hand.
She is a lot shorter than Randy, and plump with curly
gray hair, a round face and glasses. To Michael she
looks like the picture of Santa's wife he has seen. She is
wearing a sweater with a kitten on it and smiling.
Michael likes her instantly and feels at home near her.

"We found this little guy while we were out in the woods, heard him crying. Apparently, he got lost and said something about his parents not waking up and a hurt car. So, I figured he was in a car accident on route 24." Randy said as he put Michael down on his feet. "Figured we would get the truck and head down the road to see if we could find them."

"Well you go on and do that, I will take this little man right here and get him something to eat and get him warm." she says as she takes Michael's hand. "What's your name sweetie?" she asks him.

"Michael George Dunning," he says back confidently, "but mommy and daddy call me Mikey."

"Well Mikey, can I call you Mikey?" she asks, and he nods his head in approval. "Well Mikey, Randy and Adam are going to look for your parents and we will get you all fixed up okay?" She doesn't wait for an answer but looks at her sons Randy and Adam, "Adam go get Brady so he can look Michael over and when he is done with that, he can go with you in case his parents need his assistance. He is a doctor after all."

"Yes ma." the men replied in unison.

Chapter 4.

1.

"Michael!" They yelled in unison as they trekked
through the woods looking for their little boy. Silence
was all that responded.

"Where is he?" she pleaded to her husband but more so
to the world around them. "Dear God, where is he?"

He hears her but says nothing. He knows she is asking
that question as a coping mechanism and not truly
expecting an answer, just hoping one appears. He
himself is getting angrier every second that passes. He is
getting angry at himself for the accident, angry at her
parents for changing the holiday schedule, her for
asking to go to her parents, and even angry at his son,
his 4-year-old sweet little boy with the infectious smile,
for leaving the car in the first place. He pushes the
thought out of his head. He doesn't want to feel angry
at his son and now feels slightly guilty for feeling angry.
He thinks of what she would think of him if she knew
how he felt right now. Would she tell him it's all right,

it's going to be alright, or would she blame and hate him as much as he blames and hates himself?

"Michael!" He yells, this time louder and more forceful. In the background he can hear the cars open door alert system, *Ding*. He wonders if he can actually hear it or if he will never stop hearing it. He wonders if she hears it still too.

She can still hear the car dinging in the background and wonders if she hears the car or if that is just the sound she will hear until they find Michael, if they do find him. She hears her husband yell again. She knows he blames himself, and if she was to admit to herself, she did a little bit too. She hears him yell again, but she thinks she hears something else too, what sounded like a truck.

"Michael!" John yells, sounding even more frustrated. He starts to wonder...

"Hello?" the words cut through the woods like a sharp wind. They both instantly look towards the car, although they can't see it through the density of the woods. They both know someone is standing at the edge of the woods by their wrecked car shouting towards them. They look at each other and then turn.

"Hello!" they both yell as they start to rush back to the wrecked SUV. It seems to take forever. They didn't realize how far into the woods they traveled. When they finally broke through the tree line, they couldn't see their car or anybody. "Hello?" they yelled again. This time they heard the response clearly coming from right around the bend. "How easily they got turned around in the woods." John thought, "Would they, could they find Michael in this vast wilderness?"

2.

As the tow truck, followed by a large SUV rounded the bend, the three brothers could tell right away what happened. As the vehicle came around the 1st bend of the long curve, there was a large branch in the road. The driver must have swerved to miss the branch but lost control of the vehicle due to the rain and wet road and hit a large tree just off the side of the road.

When Randy, who was driving the tow truck, saw the front end of the SUV, he knew right away it was totaled. He has owned the garage and tow service in town for the last 15 years and had been working there since he was 16 for Mr. Jameson, before he bought it when Jameson retired. He was glad they went to town and got his truck - they were going to need it.

Adam didn't mind driving the large vehicle, but he did mind driving his eldest brother. Adam was the youngest of three brothers and two sisters, and was still treated like the baby of the family, even though he was 27 years old. Adam still lived with his parents and was a deputy sheriff. He had been on that road many times because of accidents and when he saw the car hugging the tree like a long-lost friend, he thought maybe Mikey's parents didn't make it.

If Adam was the baby, then Brady was the favorite. Brady was 37 years old, married with 2 kids and ran the only doctor's office in town. As Brady saw the wrecked car, he thought that if they were wearing their seatbelts, and the air bags functioned properly, there could be minimal injuries, most likely head at that.

3.

As the three brothers approached the remains of Mikey's car –as they had come to think of it - they realized no one was in the vehicle, which meant that the parents woke up and realized their son had gone missing. They all looked at each with worry on their faces. "Do you guys think someone stopped and picked them up?" Randy asked.

"We would have passed them on the road from town I would think." Adam said confidently. The boys had gone to town to get Randy's tow truck and Adam knew there was only one way into town from here.

"What if they went the other direction? I mean, Miller City is only 45 minutes that way." Randy argued, pointing in the opposite direction from where they came.

"Yeah, but they would have got cell service back just 10 minutes into that drive and would have called 911. We would have heard about it. Look their phones are gone. More than likely they wandered into the woods to look for Mikey and cell service." Adam concluded. As Adam finished, they all heard a faint sound in the distance that sounded like someone yelling Michael. That sound confirmed Adam's hypothesis of what took place.

"Hello!" they all three yelled back, towards the woods. When they heard the woods respond in kind, they smiled at each other. A little while later they saw a young couple, tattered and bleeding coming around the north bend of the curve.

4.

"Hey folks, is this your car?" Adam inquires. The other two men roll their eyes and think to themselves; *"deputy Adam is on the case."*

"Yes." The man replies, "we are..."

"looking for your son, about so tall?" Adam lets his hand flay near his knee, "4 years old, and goes by the name Mikey Dunning?" Adam finishes for the man.

"Yes, dear God yes! Is he alright?" the woman says almost shouts.

"He is fine." this time it was Brady's turn to talk.

"Me and my younger brother Adam found him in the woods a little over an hour ago. My name is Randy by the way." he says.

Brady reaches his hand out to the couple and the man takes it. "John Dunning and this is my wife Allison."

"I'm Brady, and I am the doctor around these parts. I already examined Mikey and he is doing just fine. He is as safe as can be back at our family house where he is enjoying a Thanksgiving feast. Now, I need to look you two over. I can see you suffered a head wound so I need to examine you, ok?"

"Can we go see Mikey first?" Allison said a little calmer now. "I just want to check on him myself."

"We will in just a bit. That's Randy's tow truck over there. Randy and Adam are going to remove the branch from the road and hook up your car. Adam is a deputy sheriff and said we must clean this up so no one else gets in an accident. While they are doing that, I will give you guys the once over, then we will head back to the house to check on Mikey, ok?" Brady said in his bedside manner voice.

Comment [Ma]: Please revise phrase.

5.

As John was being examined by, "Oh God what did he say his name was?" Allison thought. "Brady yeah, Brady", she watched as the other two men dragged the large branch out of the road. She thought it would have taken a car or truck to move that. By the time they got the branch to side of the road, it was her turn and she could hear the one man start his tow truck up.

John was given the all clear by Brady and wanted to help the two men. It was his car after all, and he felt responsible for them missing the holiday with their family. He was also extremely grateful that these men were out here helping them and that they helped Mikey. They told them about how they found Mikey wandering in the woods, scared and crying. He couldn't wait to wrap his arms around his son and let him know everything would be alright. Even without them telling him, John could tell they were brothers. They all three looked alike and had that same big, wide bodied country boy build to them. Adam was the smallest, and John swears he stood at least 6'3' or 6'4' and outweighed him by 50 lbs. or better. He had to admit to himself that maybe he was wrong about country living - or livin as they said - all these years.

Once they had the car hooked up and pulled away from the tree, they picked up all the bigger pieces of the wreck and put them in the back of the totaled car. Adam had pulled a broom off the tow truck and swept the road clear of debris. Then they loaded up, Adam and Randy in the tow truck and the Dunning's with Brady in the large SUV. As they headed back to the boy's house Brady filled the Dunning's in on who was awaiting them when they got to the house.

Chapter 5.

1.

They can't see the house as they pull off the highway onto what seems like a dirt road. After a winding trip through the woods, they go around a curve and into a large clearing as the dirt road turns to gravel. There they got their first view of the big house.

Allison gasped as she took the large colonial in for the first time. "Oh God, this house is beautiful!" she heard John exclaim and thought that was an understatement. The house was at least three stories on one end. The left side of the house boasted a bay window, two upstairs windows, and a small semi-circle window towards the top that Allison figured was an attic window. The other end had two windows facing the driveway, one on top of the other. There were three window dormers sticking out from the slanted roof in-between the two ends of the house. The house had a green vinyl siding which made Allison think this house would be very hard to find in the summertime when the trees were full of green leaves.

The vehicles stopped in front a set of wide steps that led up to a large friendly front porch. The porch had three pillars and an old-style swing at the one end in front of a large window. Windows surrounded the door frame. The front door opened, and they saw an older man step out. The man was easily in his sixties but could still move with relative ease. He was large like the boys and Allison knew he was their father. She could still see some red hair in his mostly grey beard and balding head. The boys all looked just like him. It was almost like seeing him age from a young man to an older man one at a time. As he stepped further out, a shorter, plump woman around his age stepped out behind him. She had a broad face and gray hair and was smiling from ear to ear.

2.

Ding, ding. As they open the doors to the vehicles Allison hears that sound again. It rises through all the other sounds and right into her brain, causing her fear to rise along with it. It was almost like the sound was warning her against danger, like an alarm. *Ding, ding.*

"Hello! Welcome to our home. I hear you guys had a rough go today but it's all over know. Come in, come, in." the plump woman said., "My name is Marge. This is Alvin and you already know the boys. Come in out of the cold and meet the rest of the family."

Ding, ding. Allison swears she can still hear the sound. She looks back and sees all the car doors are closed. She wonders if she will hear that sound for the rest of her life. *Ding, ding.*

3.

John walked up the steps quickly and held his hand out to the large patriarch. As the man shook his hand he said to himself *'My God this guy could give Superman one hell of a fight.'* "My name is John, and this is my wife Allison," he said out loud. "We understand your boys found our son and brought him here. We are eternally grateful and would love to see him now."

"Oh, my yes!" Marge said, "As a mother I totally understand, Brady would you take them upstairs, I put Mikey in your old room."

4.

As they climbed the stairwell, a sense of dread came over them, as if death itself awaited them on the second floor of the beautiful country house.

Ding, ding. John could hear that sound clear as a bell, now a warning bell. It was almost as if the universe, no the house was trying to warn them about something. Telling them to leave, to run away as fast as they could and not look back. John decided right there they would collect Mikey and leave as quickly as possible. *Ding, ding.*

When they got to the top of the stairs, they could see three doors, all closed. John started to head toward the farthest one away. In the movies it was always the farthest one away.

"John?" Brady said with a quizzical look on his face, "It's this one." Brady opened the door to the bedroom closest to the stairwell. This eased John's fears a bit and he thought "I guess this isn't a movie". As the three entered the room they could hear his soft breathing and see him lying there all cuddled under the blanket. He had the blanket pulled all the way to his ears and only the top of his blond head was exposed.

Allison was instantly calmed as she whispered to her husband "All bundled up, just like at home."

"The little guy was plum wore out and fell asleep shortly after we gave him something to eat." Brady said. "Look, I know you guys are anxious, but he had a long day and you can clearly see he is fine, so why don't we let him rest? Besides supper will be done soon. We can eat and then come get him for dessert."

Mikey's parents looked at each other and then back to the bed where their little boy lay sleeping, watching the blanket move rhythmically with his soft breathing and nodded in agreement. They went back downstairs where the rest of their gracious hosts were waiting for them.

5.

"Where's Mikey?" Marge said, greeting them at the bottom of the stairs.

"He was sleeping so peacefully; we didn't have the heart to wake him." Allison responded with a soft smile. "I was wondering if you have a phone we could use? I wouldn't ask but there seems to be no cell service and my parents will be expecting us in a couple hours. I didn't want them to worry."

"Sorry we don't have a phone. The phone company hasn't seen fit to come out this far yet," Alvin replied, "And from what I've heard, Verizon plans to put a cell tower in nearby, but that's at least a year away."

"How far is town?" John asked, "I hate to impose further, but if someone could give us a ride into town then we could call them and let them know everything is alright."

"Oh, about a half an hour east of here, give or take." Alvin answered.

"Well, supper will be done soon. Why don't we wait till after everyone eats, then we will run you into town to call your folks," Marge said.

"Besides, Mikey could use the rest." Brady added.

John looked at Allison and then his phone. He wasn't looking for service, just at the time. "If this is the right time then we got at least a couple hours before they start missing us, maybe a little longer with the weather. We could eat then go to town."

"Yeah, I suppose." Allison said hesitantly. "A couple of hours."

"Then it's settled. We'll eat then take you to town, you can make your call, and Randy might even have a loaner he can give ya to use to get you home." Brady said.

"Thank you, thank you very much" Allison said with the first sign of hope in her voice since they came down the stairs, "You said supper is almost done. Is there anything I can help with?"

"Oh no, you're our guest. I wouldn't hear of it. Plus, you all have already had such a harrowing day." Marge said.

"No, please let me help. You guys have already helped us beyond imagination, and besides I feel I need to do something. It's a way for me to repay your kindness, at least a little." Allison paused, "I insist." she added a moment later.

"If I know my wife, she won't be happy till you let her help." John said.

"Well fine" Marge said smiling. "I could use the company anyways. Brady take John out back. We will be in the kitchen finishing up supper."

"Brady, John, why don't we go out back with the rest of the family and let these ladies work their magic." Alvin said more commanding than asking. John could tell even though he was smiling and cordial, this was a man who was used to getting his way.

As they walked through the kitchen towards the back door, John could hear Marge giving Allison instructions on what to do. He was the last to go through the door but before he did, he stopped and looked back at his wife who was busy mixing flour to make a dough he believed was for rolls. He smiled at her, even though she was too busy to notice, and thought how much nicer this Thanksgiving was going to be now. *Ding, Ding.* The sound of the oven going off brought him back to reality. He shut the door on his way out.

6.

As Allison was mixing the dough for the rolls, she couldn't believe there were people that still made their own. She heard the pitter patter of little feet coming down the set of stairs that ended on the other side of the kitchen. When she looked up, she half expected and hoped to see her son bounding down the steps, but instead she saw an adorable little girl about the same age as Mikey. Standing there at the bottom of the stairs just staring at her.

"Now where have you been and what have you been up to?" Allison heard Marge say, "You better not have woken that little boy up. We told you to leave him alone. I would hate to have to fan your butt on a holiday and with guests around."

"I wasn't bothering nobody, Gamma, I swear." The little girl said looking back and forth between the two women nervously. "I just went upstairs to go potty."

Marge looked at her suspiciously and asked, "And what pray tell is wrong with the one right over there?"

Without hesitation the little girl answered her gamma, "It was out of paper."

"Mmhmm, well then I guess that is a problem, now isn't it?" Allison saw the firm look on Marge's face fade away into a smile as she responded to the little girl." Now let's not be rude. Come over here and meet this lady."

The little girl jumped off the bottom step and onto the kitchen floor and hurriedly walked over to Allison. "My name is Rosalie. You can call me Rosy for short." Rosalie said with her hand outstretched. "Your Mikey's mom isn't ya?"

"Yes, my name is Allison, you can call me Ally for short." she said.

"You can do no such thing. This is Mrs. Dunning and her husband is Mr. Dunning." Marge interjected.

"Yes ma'am. Nice to meet ya Mrs. Dunning." Rosy said.

"Nice to meet you too Rosy. You know you have almost the same hair color as my little boy." Allison said.

"Yeah, I know, I met him already." Rosy replied. The older woman laughed.

"Now you go on outside. Everyone else is already out there." Marge said through her chuckles.

"She is so adorable." Allison said to Marge as the little girl closed the door behind her.

"And don't think she don't know it." Marge said as the two ladies laughed again. Allison had a thought she instantly felt guilty for having. She thought this was going to be a better Thanksgiving than it had set out to be.

Ding, ding. The bottom part of the double oven was letting them know it was hot enough to bake the rolls.

7.

When John closed the door behind him, he could see a big backyard and the woods behind it. Somewhere on the other side of those trees there is the road that they were driving down just an hour or so ago. In those trees is where this family found his son.

In the yard, he could see Randy and Adam plus a young woman and three kids playing football. He watched as Brady left the porch to join the game. On the back porch was another young woman who was very pregnant, sitting and watching them have fun. You could tell a part of her wanted to be out there and another part was having fun just watching them play.

"John, I would like you to meet Randy's wife Caroline." Alvin said introducing them, "And Carol this is John, Mikey's dad. "

"Nice to meet you." they both said at the same time and then they both laughed a little.

"Out there playing is Marcy who is Adam's wife, Brady's Gabrielle - we call her Gabby - and Anthony, Randy and Carol's boy. As you can see, they have another one on the way. We are all hoping it's a girl. The other boy is Terrance or Terry, he belongs to Adam." Alvin said.

John couldn't help but notice he said Adam, and not Adam and Marcy. He couldn't help but wonder if Terry was from a previous relationship. He also noticed that Brady had no significant other present. He wanted to ask but thought better of it. His mom didn't raise him to be rude.

Alvin saw the quizzical look on his face and answered his questions without him asking them. "Terry is from a girl Adam got pregnant in high school. She ran off a couple years ago and left the boy with Adam to take care of. It was for the best; she wasn't ready to be a mom and didn't have a good family support system at home. And Brady's wife is a nurse at the local hospital and is working today. She will be here later, but I doubt you will still be here when she arrives." Alvin saw John's face relax and he realized he liked John. Most people would have asked but John was raised right, and he respected that.

Just as Alvin was finishing up, they heard a door shut behind them. As they turned, John saw this adorable blonde-haired little girl standing behind them. "Now this is Rosalie, my little Rosy." Alvin said with a smile so big. He was beaming and John knew this was a tight knit family and his host Alvin loved them all, especially this one. "Rosy is Adam and Marcy's little one. She was born premature and actually died for a few seconds when she was born." Alvin said. John swears he saw Alvin's eyes get a little glossy when he said this. "Rosy this is John Dunning."

"Nice to meet you Rosy. You can call me John." he said.

"Not according to Gamma, I can't." she said as the men laughed. "Well, it was nice to meet you too, but can I get by? I really want to play some football."

"By all means." John said as he turned and bowed, gesturing his arm towards the others playing in the backyard.

"Go have fun and whip them all." Alvin said.

"You have a beautiful family, Alvin." John said.

"Thank you and so do you." Alvin said. "We really are glad to have you here for dinner. We have a tradition in this family and your family is helping to keep that tradition alive."

"What tradition is that?" John asked.

"Well, let's sit down and I will tell you all about it." Alvin said.

"You're gonna love this story. I never get tired of hearing it." Caroline said.

8.

"In 1788, my ancestors were traveling with Ebenezer Sprout through the area. As Sprout and the rest of the pioneer group set up the first settlement in Ohio at Marietta, my great-great-great-great-great-great-grandfather Archibald, and grandmother Eunice, decided that they wanted to continue west. About a few weeks after departing on their own, they and a small group that continued with them came upon this grove of trees. There was a natural creek running through the area and they felt this was the best spot for them. So, they set up camp and started building houses. In fact, the small section that makes up the living room is the original house they built. The woods you see are the same woods they hunted for food in." Alvin pointed towards the woods as he said that. "Now you see, when they got settled it was early October. Thanksgiving wasn't around just yet, but the group usually gathered for meals. As a community they ate together and took care of each other. They shared just about everything. That's how they survived. See, they couldn't just go to the local grocery store for food, and they had just arrived and didn't have time to plant and grow food, so they hunted. Well, that first winter was early and harsh, Game was scarce, and they did what they could. One night, according to my grandmother, a storm was raging so bad that you couldn't see your hand in front of your face." Alvin leaned back in his chair and you could tell he was contemplating how to tell the rest of his story. John looked at him, he was staring towards the woods as if he was looking into the past himself.

"According to family legend," Alvin said leaning forward in his chair and looking directly into John's eyes, "They were starving. Only two families were left. Some went back to Marietta and some died from disease and starvation. They didn't have much food and the Wyatt family that lived just down the road had even less. Archie went out and braved the weather to get to the Wyatts and bring them back to eat. When he got there, they had run out of wood and were not only starving but freezing as well. He brought them back here, fed them and got them warmed up. Shortly after they signed over their land and headed back to Marietta. By the next year, they had plenty of food and people had started to settle around them again." Alvin finished, "So you see, helping out people on Thanksgiving is an old family tradition for us, and a tradition that we have kept almost every year. Well, as often as we could that is."

"That is one a hell of a story." John said, "It truly is amazing what people had to do to survive back then."

"You only know the half of it." Alvin laughed.

While the two men shared a small laugh, the door opened and they saw Marge step out onto the porch, "Supper's ready." she bellowed.

Chapter 6.

1.

John was the last one to enter the dining room. As everyone started to take their seats, he saw the enormous feast that was laid before them. On the table was all sorts of different foods: candied yams, mashed potatoes, gravy, rolls, peas, corn, cranberry sauce, stuffing, turkey, and what looked like a pork roast. He has had these types of food on Thanksgiving for years but never displayed like this. In his home it was always buffet style and at Allison's the food was prepped in the kitchen by the cook and brought out on plates by the staff. He had only seen this type of display in movies and on T.V.

He noticed the only open chair was in-between Brady and Randy, right across from Allison so he maneuvered himself behind the chair. He noticed the children sat at another table at the end and already had their plates prepared for them. When he looked at Rosy, he realized he had forgotten about Mikey. "Hey, shouldn't we go wake Mikey?"

"Oh, let him sleep. The rest will do him good." Marge said smiling. John could tell she was happy and proud of the feast that she had prepared for her family. "Don't worry there is plenty. We will save him a plate."

"Yeah, let him sleep." Allison added. "it'll be ok."

After everyone was seated except him and Alvin, John cleared his throat. "Can I have everyone's attention please? I just wanted to thank you all for your continued generosity. If it wasn't for this family," John said fighting back tears, "God only knows where my own family would be right now. I have no way to repay your kindness, except to say thank you from the bottom of our hearts and if there is anything we can do, don't hesitate to ask." John sat down as everyone around him was thanking him for the words.

Allison just smiled at him and beamed with pride. She never loved him more than at this moment. She loved how he was as honest with people as he was with his emotions. He never feared to be seen as unmanly if the people he cared about knew how much he truly cared.

2.

As Alvin listened to John's words and saw the emotion on the man's face, he felt a deep sympathy for him. He liked John, Allison, and Mikey and felt bad for all that they had to endure on this day. He was even happier however that they were here to help carry on the 200 plus year tradition.

"Thank you, John." Alvin said. "Now with this feast before us and everyone seated, let's begin. Please everyone bow your heads and let us pray and thank God for this day." They all did so, even Allison and John who were not religious people did it out of respect for their hosts. "Dear God, we want to thank you for this food we are about to receive. We want to thank you for the health and prosperity of our family and loved ones. We want to thank you for bringing the Dunning family into our lives on this day so we can celebrate this holiday with them and continue our long family tradition. In your name we pray, Amen." Alvin said concluding the prayer. "Before we eat, I do want to add something. John, Allison we are grateful you are here. It is our pleasure and honor for you to sit with us as we celebrate this day."

'Thank you." John and Allison said in unison.

"Now, let's eat." Alvin said as people started to dig in and put food on their plates. Some were eating as they were gathering but everyone got a little of everything. As they ate, everyone talked and laughed. Alvin looked at his wife Marge and they beamed together at the joyous occasion happening around them. As people finished eating and the conversation quieted down, Alvin looked at John and Allison. "Did you two try the special dish?"

"Which one is that?" Allison asked.

"The roast right in front of you." Alvin said. "It's a traditional dish that goes all the way back to that harsh winter meal I told John about."

"Oh yes, John told me that story during dinner. What an incredible tale." Allison said. "But no, I haven't tried it yet."

"Well please do. After all it is tradition and this family is big on tradition." Alvin said. "Have some too John."

"Well if it is tradition, why not. It does look good." John said as he held his plate out and Allison cut the meat and placed some on John's plate then her own. Alvin watched intently as the two cut the meat and ate. "Wow, that is good. It is kind of like pork in the texture, but the meat is really sweet. What is it?" John asked, unaware that Randy and Brady were standing behind him, and Adam behind Allison.

"Oh my God, this is so good!" Allison exclaimed. "Seriously, what is this?"

"Well, first off it is an old recipe, but the meat is fairly young. See that's the trick, the younger they are the sweeter the meat. As they age the meat gets tougher, still good but a different taste. That one there is aged around 4 years." Alvin said.

Ding, ding, ding.

A sense of dread washed over them. John suddenly felt sick to his stomach. He looked at his wife as she was looking at her plate in confusion and fear. He realized at this moment that they never actually saw Mikey since they had been here. "Uh, I, uh need to go get Mikey." John said with fear pouring out of his voice.

"Well, technically Mikey is already here." Alvin said as his hand gestured towards the plate of meat that John and Allison had just ate from. "You could say that he will always be with you." Alvin said as the whole family chuckled at the joke.

John looked at his wife who was horror struck. He stood from the table quickly, enraged and in denial of what he was hearing. "WHERE IS MY SON?" he yelled, as the two men grabbed his arms and he felt a sharp pain of a needle enter his neck. He saw Adam stick a needle in Allison's neck. *This can't be happening,* he said to himself. He was thinking "I ate my son." Then everything went black.

Chapter 7.
1.

Ding, ding, ding.

Allison opened her eyes to the sound of danger in her head. The room she was in was dark. There was a little light coming from her right and she was upside down. She looked around and saw John hanging upside down next to her and he was naked. That is when she realized she was naked as well. She suddenly felt very cold and very afraid.

Allison tried to remember what had happened, but her mind was foggy, and she was having trouble focusing. Then she heard a door open and heard a woman say, "Don't be too long, the little ones want to hear the story." she knew that voice. It was Marge, Marge the plump older woman that helped them after the accident. The one that took care of Mikey after her boys found him in the woods. Mikey...now it was all coming back. They killed Mikey and ate him. They ALL ate him. They fed them their own son and laughed about it. "Don't worry this won't take too long, I'm just gonna bleed them. Reading that story is very important, it's tradition and you know I'm a stickler for tradition." she heard a male voice say. Alvin; his name rose in her like hot lava. She saw a white fluorescent light come on and it lit up the entire room. It was tiled white like a bathroom with a drain on the floor in between her and John. She looked and saw John was tied with a rope and hung on a hook between his feet, his arms dangling below and almost touching the floor. She figured she must be hung in the same manner. She heard footsteps descending the stairs and realized she had but a few seconds. She then started to swing her body and jerk herself hoping that she would get off the hook somehow and then figure out a way to escape.

2.

Alvin smiled as he descended the stairs to the basement. He could hear someone trying desperately to get off the hook. In all his years he has seen many people try to get off the hook but can only remember one person doing it. He had just turned 13 and his dad felt it was time to teach him how to prepare the traditional meal. The boy was sixteen, a whole three years older than him. When they hung him, he didn't get the rope all the way in the hook but on it, so the boy was able to jerk himself free. However, when he came off the hook, he ended up breaking his neck and dying anyways. His dad just laughed and re-hung him and proceeded like normal. The only thing he said to Alvin was always make sure the rope was inside the hook; a lesson he never forgot again. At that moment Alvin missed his father more than ever. It was always tough around the holidays.

"I see someone is awake." Alvin said as he rounded the corner at the bottom of the stairs. He looked at Allison hanging there, naked, and thought she was a remarkably beautiful woman. "Try as you will, you won't get off that hook. It will just tire you out. In the long run it makes no difference to me." he said as he crossed the room to the counter where the tools he needed sat in waiting. After they had found Mikey, he came down there and cleaned the tools in preparation. After Mikey had fallen asleep he used them to kill the boy and carve him up. He was small and not much meat, but he was delicious, Alvin thought. He then hosed the room down and cleaned the tools again so they would be ready for Mikey's parents.

The tools he was referencing was a set of knives. This set was over 200 years old and was the original set used in that first meal. They had been repaired and preserved over the years, and only brought out on special occasions like this. The different knives had different purposes. The smaller knife was used to skin the meat, while the long skinny one was used to slash the throat and cut open the abdomen and empty the abdominal cavity. There was another knife that was used to separate flesh from bone, and yet another one to cut through bone, mainly the ribs. There was a heavier one used for carving the meat that looked like an old version of a cleaver. Alvin looked at these tools and remembered the first time Brady helped him. In fact, he believed that being down there during those times was what got Brady interested in becoming a doctor.

Alvin picked up the long skinny knife, turned and headed for the Dunnings. "You know the story I told your husband was true. I only left out the part that after bringing the Wyatts here, my ancestor Archibald, proceeded to kill them and use their bodies to nourish the family through the next couple of weeks. By then the storm had passed and they were able to hunt and find game again."

"Why are you doing this? What did we do? Whatever it was, we're sorry. Please don't do this." Allison cried. "Please you can let us go, we won't say anything, even about Mikey. We will tell people he disappeared, that after the accident he was just gone. No one needs to know. Who would we tell anyway? Your son is a police officer!"

"Oh, I can't let you go, and I already told you why it's tradition." Alvin answered. "I will tell you this. You surprised me, being the first to wake up and all. I was expecting John to wake up. I even bet Brady he would. Now I owe Brady a five spot." Alvin approached John and knelt down. *Ding, ding, ding.* He held the blade of the knife on his throat near his right ear. Allison looked on in anguish as Alvin pushed the blade into John's throat and drew it across the rest to the other side. The blade didn't hesitate, and Alvin didn't have to use much pressure as the knife cut deep into the man's throat as easily as cutting butter. He saw John's eyes open as the blade entered his neck. He saw the confusion and fear turn to pain. He watched as John fought and his body jerked after the cut was made. He watched as the blood ran down his face, covering it in a crimson mask. He watched as John's body slowed down and quit jerking as the life left him, until he didn't move at all. He heard Allison scream at first. He heard it fade into a whimper as John died. He heard her crying still.

When the blood flow slowed to a trickle Alvin walked back up to John's corpse. He inserted the knife in John's belly button and sliced him to his sternum. As he did this the organs inside John's body fell out and landed on the floor with a loud, wet, sickening thud. Alvin then wiped the blade clean with a towel that hung from the front of his brown leather apron.

"Darlin I have no doubt that you believe you wouldn't tell, but eventually you would. I have a family to protect and provide for. In all my years doing this, there is always someone who begs and pleads and tries to make a deal, but we didn't survive this long letting people go." Alvin lectured. "So no, I won't be letting you go."

"The police will come, even if your son is a cop." she threatened. "They will come, and they will stop you."

"Yes, someone will come and the local sheriff, who is the only law in this county, will say no one has seen you and he will lead an investigation. The local lab is controlled by the local physician: Brady, and then your vehicle will be looked for. They will ask the only junkyard owner, who is also the only mechanic and owns the only garage in the area - Randy. And yes my son Adam is a Deputy Sheriff and will assist in the investigation, but it will be led by the County Sheriff, Me."

"Why?" she begged, "for Christ's sake just tell me why!"

"Cause it's tradition." Alvin replied coldly. With those words all hope left her, and she knew that not only would her and her family die, but no one would ever know what happened to them.

Ding, ding, ding.

She felt the cold blade against her throat, she felt the pain as Alvin pushed it into her flesh and drew it across her neck. She felt her body writhe as it fought against dying. She felt the blood enclose her face as her life force drained from her. The only thought she had was that she was sorry. She was sorry for making them go to her parents for Thanksgiving. She was sorry for leading her husband and her son to their deaths. She thought of her husband and her son. "John, Mikey, I love you. Momma is coming baby, momma is coming," was her last thought. Her eyes got dark and she saw, felt or thought no more.

The End.

Christmas

Dear Santa

Dear Santa,

Let me start by saying that I am not some whimsical child believing in some fat magic man that once a year brings toys to little boys and girls worldwide. I am in fact an adult who is using this as an outlet, a form of confession. After all, I hear confession is good for the soul. I don't begrudge those who indulge in this fantasy as I like to live out my own fantasies as often as I can, and those fantasies that I have lived out and the one I am planning, are the reasons for writing this.

I recently saw a documentary that said that very little of these Santa letters actually get read and most end up in an incendiary somewhere. So, because of this I am taking a calculated risk to fulfill these needs for confession. Some people indulge in similar fantasies, as I like to tease authorities, but I am not that much of a risk taker, so I shall stay in the shadows and continue my good works in silence, with the exception of this letter of course. Maybe I will continue to write them on a yearly basis if this works out, but for now where to start? The beginning I suppose. As the great novelist Charles Dickens once wrote "I am born".

I was born to an upper middle-class family and grew up in one of the fanciest apartment buildings in the city. I had a nanny who also served as the maid and cooked for the household until I was about 10

years old, and then she ran off
with my father. I hated my father
for taking her away from me and
leaving me alone with my mother.
Still do.

My mother was insufferable when
sober and worse when she drank,
and she always drank. On really
troubling evenings she would play
the song "Goodnight Sweetheart"
by The Spaniels and come into my
room and beat me. As she hit me
repeatedly with a leather belt, she
would blame me for him leaving,

for looking like him every day, and making her life miserable since the day I was born. It was no secret that my mother didn't want much to do with me and that, in her mind, I prevented her from having fun, hence the reason for the nanny. So, I guess in a way I was responsible.

She chose that song for a couple of reasons: one because it was the first song my mother and father ever danced to; and two because she would play it loud enough so the neighbors couldn't hear the beatings. They all knew anyway. This continued until I was 16, well at least that's where things changed.

On my 16th birthday, I received a card from my father. In it was a long letter about becoming a man and what that meant. Like I would listen to a man who I haven't seen in 6 years and have only briefly talked to a few times, usually on my birthday and Christmas. However, also in this letter was a check for $50,000.

He said it was for me to buy a brand-new car for my birthday. My mother decided that she was going to buy me a car as well, so I put back the money my father sent me. My mother found the letter my father had sent me later that night and I remember clearly hearing the song come on.

When I first heard the music playing that night, I knew exactly what was coming. I remember lowering my pants and leaning over the bed. When she came in, she was yelling and calling me names as usual, except this night she had forgotten her belt, so she decided to hit me with her hand. As she leaned over to smack my bare ass, she noticed that my penis was hard. To put it in a more rudimentary term – she lost her shit. She started screaming and calling me a pervert like my father. She said I was just like him, I was getting angry, I was nothing like him. She started smacking me in my head. As I stood up, she smacked me in my face. I looked at her and I saw anger leave and fear creep into her eyes. I stood a whole foot taller than her now as she looked up at me. I grabbed her and threw her on my bed. That night I became a man, no THE man. That night I removed all authority from my mother and took it for myself. That night I became the man of the house.

After the night of my 16th birthday the dynamic between me and my mother changed. She still drank, but she cowered away from me instead of bullying me. I could say that the events that took place that night never repeated themselves, but they did. Not at first, but not until 4 months later did a reoccurrence happen, and then it would happen with greater frequency. It wasn't always violent sometimes, it just happened.

I was not well thought of amongst my peers. I had money, good looks, was physically fit, and had a high level of intelligence but I was socially awkward. I didn't have friends; some might say I was withdrawn and because of that I was lonely and so was she. She was still very attractive, but her unpleasant disposition and her constant drinking kept people at bay, so we took our anger, our loneliness, and other emotions out on each other. Did I love my mother? Yes, I did, but I hated her as well. Oh, how I longed to choke the life out of her during one of our special nights.

After one of our more harrowing special nights, I was walking home from school when a young lady who was in my class caught up with me. She and I talked for a bit and she smiled at me, a smile I had never seen directed towards me. We got along well and at one point she kissed me. I was over the moon. For the next 3 weeks we dated secretly. She didn't want anyone to know because she was very popular and was worried what her friends would think and I didn't want mother to find out. I didn't want her ruining what I

had, but she would anyways. She
always did.

On one particular Friday evening
I had told mother I was going to
the library, when in reality I was
going to an illicit rendezvous with
my lady love. When I arrived, she
was there with one of her friends
and they were both heavily drunk.
My love acted like she didn't like
me and couldn't understand what
I was doing there and tried to run
me off, but her friend had other
plans.

As I was trying to play along with my lady love and walk away, her friend came up to me and put her arms around me. She started saying things like how she never noticed how attractive I was because of how weirdly I always acted. Then she kissed me. I looked at my lady and she had an angry and astonished look on her face that I quite enjoyed. On a few different occasions she tried to get her friend to make me leave, but her friend persisted that I stay, and as the night progressed, the alcohol flowed more frequently, and the morals loosened.

Eventually we all ended up naked and doing wonderfully terrible things. But as I looked at my love's friend I grew angrier and angrier because I could tell my love was getting more than upset about what we were doing, but couldn't decide how to stop it without letting the cat out of the bag. One of the things that upset me was that if she truly cared about me, she would have stopped us, but she allowed the debauchery to continue. What happened next - and in a way my dear Mr. Claus, what has happened since - is as much their fault as it is my mother's. Of course, you do not have to worry about putting them on the naughty list anymore, now do you.

At one point during intercourse, her friend slapped me hard in the face. I quite enjoyed that, and so I then wrapped my hands around her throat and started to squeeze.

She seemed to enjoy it at first,
that was until I completely closed
off her airway. No matter how
hard she fought, I wouldn't let
go. The harder she fought the more
I enjoyed it. My lady was
screaming at me to let her go, but
I could not. I came to climax as I
felt her life slip from her body.
My lady became hysterical. I
tried to reason with her, but she
would not stop screaming. I tried
to show her how her friend would
have hurt us, how this is better,
but in the end I had to silence her
as well. Of all the things I have

done, that is the one I wish I could undo, or at least have handled a little differently.

I got dressed as both women lay there dead. I admit I was panicking. I stood there looking at them and fearing what would happen next. I clearly remember hearing a noise, although as I look back that may have been my imagination. I raced home and told my mother what I had done. I admit she surprised me. I feared that she would call the police, or better yet blackmail me into gaining control of the household back, yet she did neither. With a form of clarity she should not have been able to muster given how much she had drank that day already, she told me what to do. I went down to the caretakers shed, broke in, and stole a couple of shovels and a big bag of lye. I then drove her to where the bodies were when I left them. They were there unmolested. We picked up the bodies and put them in the car. I picked up all the trash we had created and drove to a wooded area an hour or so outside of the city. I then dug a few holes, dropped the girls in them along with the trash bag and covered them all with the lye. We left after I had finished filling in the freshly dug graves, and on our way home, we stopped at a few dumpsters and disposed of the shovels and our clothes (we had brought extra with us).

For the next few weeks pictures of the missing girls appeared, and police came and left the school many times, talking with different students and friends of theirs. I was never questioned, nor did anybody at the school even think of me as a suspect. After a few months with no arrests and obviously no real leads, I began to relax. I figured if I had been a suspect, they would have at least interviewed me by now.

My life went back to the way it was prior to my fling with my lady love and stayed that way until I went off to college. Even then, that first year at college, I was far too busy to entertain any outside activities. I returned home for summer, and my mother was a lot happier than she had been since my father had left. Apparently, she had met a man while I was away at school. She made it very clear to me that she liked this man and wanted to make it work. She still drank but now she waited until supper to start. I met him the next day as we all went to my favorite restaurant for dinner. I can honestly say, Santa, that I did not like him from the moment I laid eyes on him. Is hate at first sight a thing? Anyhow, I didn't like how he ordered my mother around and how he looked at her. He was a Neanderthal - unintelligent, handsy, and unworthy of my mother's attention. He had managed to generate a certain amount of wealth, of which is important to my mother as she likes the extravagant lifestyle. I couldn't wait till summer was over.

When I returned to college, I was still very cross with my mother for allowing that thing to come between us. I found myself roaming the

campus late one night and came
upon a young woman sitting
against a tree. She was dark
haired and obviously she had drank
enough to pass out. I removed my
shirt and the white tank top style
undershirt I preferred to wear
(commonly known as a wife-
beater). I put my outer shirt back
on and looked around. No one was
nearby. The tree was young, and
the trunk was not very thick. The
leaf-filled branches hid me from
the overhead light as I reached
around the trunk with my
undershirt. I pulled the shirt tight

against her throat and used the leverage of the tree to cut off her oxygen. Even with the alcohol, she woke up almost instantly, fighting and grasping for breath. I couldn't see her face, but she must have been frantically trying to figure out what was happening. After a moment she quit struggling and lay still. I felt better, but not satisfied. I decided from then on if I was to ever kill again, I would look into their eyes and watch as the light left them. However unsatisfied, I was aroused because of the night's activity, so I went

back to my dorm room and
masturbated. I was lucky because
I had no roommate that first year,
but that was about to change.

About two weeks after my nightly
encounter I returned to my dorm
one day after absorbing the local
flavor. As I walked in, a stranger
was laying on the previously
unoccupied bunk across from mine.
As I entered, he stood and
introduced himself. My new roomy
was about 2 inches taller than me,
blonde and was apparently there to

play football. Like any American male, I knew of the game but had no desire to watch or view it, or any game to be honest. Sports, as it were, was not my "thing". I felt that the arrival of my new friend would dampen my nighttime activities. But this fear, I would find out later on was unwarranted, as for the first two months he used our room as more of a storage unit until he moved out completely as he joined a frat house. About two days after his arrival he asked if I heard about this girl that had died in the commons. I of course said no, and he regaled me with the tale of how a young co-ed died from choking on her own vomit after getting drunk and passing out against a tree. He told me that campus security was going to crack down on parties to try and prevent this from happening again. I almost smiled and had to actively turn my head and act as if this news was upsetting. I decided however to take my nocturnal outings off-campus. The town was much larger and would be more difficult to be seen. As it was over the next three years, I ended the lives of seven women, all of them drunken whores who didn't want to live any longer. I was cleaning out the riffraff and putting to rest those who were a stain on society. I was performing a civic service that everyone knew needed to be done, but refused to act.

After I graduated, I returned home. My mother was drinking heavily again as was her male companion. He had taken up residence with my mother at our apartment and wedding preparations had begun. I would soon find out that he had lost his job, was never wealthy, and was using my mother financially. I would also find out that she had confronted him about it, and he had beaten her. Thus, now he beats her frequently. I tried to interfere once and was reminded that I was not a fighter. Yes, I know Santa, why should I care since I too have struck my mother and worse. But I do love my mother. Above all the resentment and hatred, there is love. Plus, I never liked him anyway. I could

not kill him without raising
suspicions upon me or my mother,
so one night I installed a hidden
video camera and not long after he
began to beat her. I recorded the
whole thing and gave it to the
police. He was arrested and given
five years in jail. He got out about
a year later and then one night I
crept into his crappy apartment
and sliced his throat as he slept.

I was investigated but never
charged. There was no evidence
and no witnesses, plus since I have

no record, they didn't believe I was capable of such an act. The detective in charge of the investigation told me that investigating me was just a formality since I was the one to send him to jail and that he believed it was one of the dozen gangs he owed money to. After the investigation ended, my mother, drunk as usual, came into my room and rewarded me for protecting her. Apparently, she didn't truly hate the relationship we had prior to my leaving for college, and said that after I left, she felt very

alone. She would be dead shortly
after that night, though not by my
hand. She died from Alcoholic
ketoacidosis apparently, she had
been suffering from it in silence for
some time.

It's true that I had fantasized
about killing her, about a world
without her since I was a child,
but I also loved her, and her death
grieved me desperately. I was
angry that she cared so little as to
harm herself and to allow herself to
die. It angered me that I was

alone in this world, but most of all it angered me that I was robbed of fulfilling my greatest desire of ending her myself. I would love to tell you Santa that I had a plan to kill her myself, but no plan existed. I guess I just figured that one day I would kill her and then most likely kill myself as well, but since she died without my assistance, I feel, no I know I must continue my civic duty.

Shortly after her funeral, I found myself in this seedy little bar near the edge of town. There was this lovely young lady with dark curly hair and a slim frame. She had dark brown eyes and looked years younger than she was, except when she smiled, and you could see the crow's feet at the edge of her lines and the deep laugh lines next to her mouth. We struck up a conversation and talked for about 20 minutes or so, but nonetheless she refuted my advances. When I returned from a restroom break, she was sitting with another man and they were openly engaging in strong displays of public affection. I left and

waited in my car for them. Before
you ask, no I was not upset at
all, in fact I was a little thrilled
at my new idea.

When the bar closed, and the
drunken love birds left the nest, I
followed them as they poorly drove
out of town. They turned down this
railroad access road and stopped
just out of sight of the highway, I
parked my vehicle along the side of
the two-lane, deserted highway
and crept through the woods. Their
windows were down, and I could

see them in the backseat as she sat on top of him. I could also see the moment he passed out while they were still engaged in the sexual activity and she got mad but decided to continue. I pulled out my dagger and moved quietly along the side of the car. I reached in, grabbed her hair and before she could say anything, I slit her throat deep almost to her spine. She bled a lot and all over him. I was waiting for him to wake up and do the same to him, but he just continued to sleep and snore through it all. I had a better idea and put the long, blood covered knife into his hand. I made sure since obtaining the knife to routinely wipe it down and to never handle it without surgical gloves on. I then found and used his cell phone to dial 9-1-1. He was given life without parole for her death. How I laughed watching the news and seeing him led away proclaiming his innocence. I even went to the courthouse a few times and sat in during his trial. How I fantasized about being on the jury, going over the crime scene photos. I wondered what they talked about

during their deliberations, how they
discussed what was before them
and how they tried in vain to figure
out what happened. During the
trial I did realize something, I
realized I was humming
"Goodnight Sweetheart" and knew
that every time I eliminated
someone, I hummed that song.

Over the course of the next three
years I eliminated four more
women and two men. Ending the
lives of the two men were nowhere
near as satisfying. However, the

young women were more than satisfying. One I carved up with a hunting knife, while another I raped and choked the life out of her. I shot one with a pistol I acquired, but felt nothing on that and realized that I am more of the hands-on type.

Just the other day I met this lovely woman at a bus stop. I helped her with her packages she had. She explained to me that she had just wrapped up her Christmas shopping. She has long, straight raven-black hair and the most beautiful greenish-blue eyes I have ever seen. I can't wait to watch the light go out in those wondrous eyes.

Well Santa I must go, I got a bus to catch.

Merry Christmas!

Acknowledgments

I would like to thank my family for the continued support in my journey to becoming a novelist. I would like to thank Amy McCarthy for her superb editing job, I know it was a daunting task. I would also like to take this time to thank you - the reader. Thank you for taking time to share my world. I hope you enjoyed the visit and come back soon.

FEEDBACK

I cannot lie that I was not filled with a certain foreboding dread while reading this. I was as livid as I was transfixed in unshaking fear and suspense. Especially the story of Mikey and his parents. A wonderfully horrific piece no doubt. I commend your effort and your radical mind. You are indeed a captivating novelist.

Made in the USA
Middletown, DE
01 October 2020